Seeds in the Desert

Seeds in the Desert

BY MENDEL MANN

Translated by Heather Valencia

A YIDDISH BOOK CENTER TRANSLATION

Yiddish Book Center
Amherst, MA 01002

978-0-9893731-7-3 (paperback)

Cover illustration by Owen Smith
Book and cover design by Michael Grinley

A Yiddish Book Center Translation

This publication was made possible with the generous support of
Righteous Persons Foundation
The Applebaum Foundation

.

Contents

Introduction   vii

Seeds in the Desert   1
The Old Jackal   18
By the Ruins of Apollonia   23
The Search for the Nabateans   30
The Dove of Nablus   35
The Lizard   40
The Mosaic of Ashkelon   46
With My Own Hands   53
The Encounter in Ramat Gan   59
Swarthy Meylekh and the Turtledove of Sharon   65
The Quiet Man of Prophets Street   71
The Ice Floe   82
Kuzma the Muzhik   88
Reflections Beside a Young Pine Tree   92
Laughter from the Skies   96
A Man in a Cloud of Dust   104
The Fiery Cross   109
Cain Laments at Night   114
The Cherry Orchard   120
A Ruined Fair   126
Yitskhok the Red   132
A Tragedy in Four Acts and an Epilogue   138
Getzl Okhlap   144
The Fallen Angel   149
The Last Scribe   156

Glossary   163

Introduction

The Writer Mendel Mann (1916–1975)

Mendel Mann was one of the last Yiddish writers to have grown up in the Jewish society of eastern Europe before the Holocaust. Even among his generation, Mann is unusual: although he started writing in Warsaw in 1938, the majority of his creative work was done after the war in the two countries where he made his postwar home, Israel and France. His oeuvre reflects the three phases of his own life: childhood and youth in the now-disappeared traditional Jewish environment, the horrors of war and persecution, and the experience of exile and re-building. The struggle for a new and meaningful existence in the fledgling state of Israel is a major focus of his work, and he confronts the ethical and emotional problems of the state with penetrating insight and psychological realism.

Mann was born in Warsaw, Poland, but he grew up in the village of Kuchary, near Płock. His father, an adherent of the Haskalah, the Jewish Enlightenment, believed in the importance of a secular European education, and Mann was educated in a Polish-language school, where his talent for painting developed. He was admitted to the Academy of Arts in Warsaw to study painting in 1938, just before war was declared. He escaped to Russia, where he worked as an educator in Tin'geshi, a remote village in Chuvashia, before enlisting in the Red Army, in which he served for the duration of the war. He took part in the battle against the Germans during the siege of Moscow and in the fall of Berlin, events that gave rise to his *Milkhome trilogye* (*War Trilogy*).

Returning to Poland after the war, he discovered that his whole family had perished during the Holocaust. He had started writing poetry before the war, and his first collection of poems, eloquently entitled *Di shtilkeyt mont* (*Silence Cries Out*), appeared in 1946. It was the first book in Yiddish to be published in postwar Poland. During the short period he spent in Łódź, Mann worked to help Jewish orphans emigrate to Israel, but soon found, especially in the wake of the pogrom of Kielce in 1946, that he could no longer bear to live in Poland. He left with his wife, Sonia, and their four-year-old son.

A short period of wandering ended when they arrived in the German city of Regensburg, where they stayed until 1948. During this period they were lodged under the protection of the American military authorities in a huge empty castle, Schloss Sulzbach, probably because Mann was in possession of sensitive information about the Soviet army. His son Zvi has vividly described the isolation he felt as a four-year-old child wandering around the huge rooms with only two hunting dogs for company. "When my father was at home in the castle, he shut himself in one room [. . .] Whenever I went in there he was very angry. He spent many hours in this room. I hated that. Writing prevented him from playing with me."

In addition to his fiction and poetry, Mann produced editorials and other articles for Regensburg's Yiddish weekly. *Der nayer moment* (*The New Moment*)—later *Undzer moment* (*Our Moment*)—ran from March 1946 until November 1947. It was printed in Hebrew characters on an old Linotype machine dating from 1886. The title echoed the major Warsaw Yiddish paper *Der moment* and symbolized the survival and renewal of Jewish life in Europe. Mann's editorials confronted the burning questions of this turbulent time: the pogroms that forced many Jews to leave Poland in 1946, the horrors of the Holocaust, the complex relationship of Jews with postwar Germany, and the hope of new life in Israel, which he saw as the only possible solution for "our homelessness, our nomadic existence" (editorial of April 3, 1947). For this reason, he bitterly castigated the shocking treatment of would-be immigrants to Palestine by the British, who turned back three ships, including the *Exodus*, in July 1947. The other nations, he lamented, remained silent at this injustice, "just as they were silent while the crematoriums were burning" (editorial of August 29, 1947). The publication of this and a number of other Yiddish journals in Germany just after the Holocaust is an extraordinary phenomenon in the history of the Yiddish press.

Mann's second book of poetry, *Yerushe* (*Heritage/Inheritance*), was published in Regensburg in 1947. The title is deeply symbolic: the poems mourn the lost heritage of Jewish life in Poland but also evoke continuity and a future inheritance for the Jewish people. For Mendel Mann this future lay in a Jewish homeland, and when the new state was declared in 1948, he and his family emigrated to Israel.

It is well known that the policy of the fledgling state was to suppress Yiddish, or *mame-loshn* (mother tongue). Yiddish was perceived as being stained with the humiliation and hopelessness of the Diaspora; modern Hebrew, the virile old-new language, represented the rebirth in freedom of a Jewish homeland. This hostility caused great distress among large numbers of Holocaust survivors, who after losing their European homes and, in most cases, many or all of their family members, now faced the extinction of their language. Like the poet Avrom Sutzkever, who had also settled in Israel, Mendel Mann had the courage and determination to pursue his creative life in Yiddish. When Sutzkever established the literary journal *Di goldene keyt* (*The Golden Chain*) in 1949, Mann became Sutzkever's colleague—as the journal's secretary and as a contributor.

Mann's literary career flourished. Despite the privations of life in the early years of the state, he was extremely productive from his arrival until his early death. He produced ten novels and a great many short stories, as well as several plays. His most ambitious work of the 1950s draws on his experiences as a Red Army officer during the war. The three volumes of his war trilogy, *Bay di toyern fun Moskve* (*At the Gates of Moscow*), *Bay der Vaysl* (*At the Vistula*), and *Dos faln fun Berlin* (*The Fall of Berlin*), were published between 1956 and 1960. (The first volume of the trilogy was published in English translation by St. Martin's Press, New York, in 1963.) The central character of the trilogy, Menakhem Issakovitsh, is, like many of the lonely individuals who people Mann's work, an alter ego of the writer himself. Through his eyes, Mann creates a vivid and broad panorama of the war, focusing on events the author himself experienced: the defense of Moscow and the terrible destruction of Warsaw, including the Jewish ghetto, during which the Red Army took no action to aid the city—an unbearable situation for a Polish Jew like Mann and his protagonist. The third volume depicts the march of the Red Army on Berlin. Mann participated in all these events and does not shrink from depicting the cruelty of the victors as well as the human misery of the defeated.

In 1961, Mann moved to Paris to work for the Yiddish newspaper *Undzer vort* (*Our Word*). There he continued writing and returned to his first love, painting, producing a large number of delicate watercolor landscapes. He became a friend of Mark Chagall, whose 1969 picture *Der dikhter Mendl Man in zayn dorf* (*The Poet Mendel Mann in His Village*) depicts the writer as a tall figure dressed in black, holding an open book and bending like a tree over a typical Chagallian village. Flames spurt from one of the houses, while a small figure with two children appears to be fleeing. In the dark, threatening sky, a couple hovers. Although the setting of this picture is reminiscent of Chagall's idyllic shtetl paintings, its darker mood reflects the recent trauma of the Jewish people. The man stares in apprehension, rather than rapture, at the viewer; the woman peers anxiously at the village below. Mann resided in Paris until his death in 1975, though he traveled widely, giving rise to stories set in locations as diverse as Texas and Australia. (See, for example, "Laughter from the Skies" on p. 96 of this collection.)

Mendel Mann's work draws on all the experiences of his adventurous life, but it cannot be pigeonholed as purely autobiographical. In all his settings—the Poland of his childhood, the war-torn cities of Moscow and Berlin, the desolate desert places of Israel—he depicts a wide diversity of human individuals, animals, and landscapes. He evokes the essential strangeness and mystery of the relationships between human beings and between human beings and the natural world.

The volume *Kerner in midber* (*Seeds in the Desert*), published in Paris in 1966, consists of forty short stories that move backward in time through the landscapes of the writer's life; the first sixteen are set in the early years of the state of Israel. Mann does not present the reader with a romanticized image but rather a subtle and nuanced view of the new nation; he depicts the fragmented, precarious nature of early Israeli society, where each person deals with his or her own personal exile, never free of the past, which continues in their lives as a living presence. He evokes the struggles of individuals to conquer the inhospitable earth and to settle in the ancient, mythic landscape that threatens to overwhelm them. He is unique among Yiddish writers in depicting with great empathy the Arabs, whose lives were irrevocably changed by the establishment of the new state.

The next twelve stories journey through Russia, Germany, America, and Australia during the last days and in the wake of the Second World War. Again the common denominators are the horrors that never relinquish their grip and the isolation of displaced individuals. Of the seven stories from this section of the book chosen for this volume, five focus penetratingly and uncomfortably on the psychological traumas and moral dilemmas that war inflicts on all who are caught up in it ("Reflections Beside a Young Pine Tree," p. 92; "Laughter from the Skies," p. 96; "A Man in a Cloud of Dust," p. 104; "The Fiery Cross," p. 109; and "Cain Laments at Night," p. 114).

The final twelve stories move further back in time, to the writer's childhood in Poland. These pieces are far from idyllic depictions: the hand of the powerful *porets*, the Polish landowner, hovers threateningly over Jewish life, and the streets of Warsaw contain Jewish gangsters as well as rabbis. Nevertheless there is a warmth in the memories of luscious green fields and forests, of a wholeness in Jewish life, and of a time when Jewish and Christian boys played happily together—a stark contrast from the underlying mood of the other two sections. The volume constitutes an inner journey from his present life in Israel right back to his origins, to Jewish Poland, where the flowering of modern Yiddish culture began.

But Mendel Mann acknowledged that with the Holocaust and the establishment of the secular Israeli state, this ancient Jewish culture of Poland had also disappeared. The volume closes with the story "The

Last Scribe." The narrator looks back to the time of his bar mitzvah, when in accordance with family tradition, his name is added to the family tree in his grandfather's ancient prayer book. His grandfather explains to him the illustrious history of this family of Torah scribes, and the thirteen-year-old boy promises his grandfather that he will follow in the footsteps of his ancestors. The narrator does indeed become a scribe, but of a very different kind: "I became a scribe of the everyday words of ordinary people." Before fleeing from the burning city of Warsaw, he looked at the family tree one last time, then left the book behind, destined for destruction. The story ends with the words: "Yesterday is destroyed like a burned forest. I walk through it alone. In my memory the tree in the old prayer book lives on."

Mann's particular style and narrative technique create the subtle nuances of the stories. The majority are related by a first-person, anonymous narrator. The reader is never certain whether these narrators are different individuals or all the same person; there is mystery about their identities. The writer who listens to the disturbing story told by the stranger in "With My Own Hands" could well be the same rootless individual who wanders aimlessly around the Bedouin market in "Seeds in the Desert" or who carries his own burden of guilt in "The Quiet Man of Prophets Street." In many stories, the first-person narrator encounters a stranger who recounts significant events of his life. Mann uses the first-person narrator of the stories—or the secondary narrator who tells his story to that anonymous "I"—as a means of evoking the different situations of isolation and anguish that characterize the uprooted individuals caught in the turmoil of war and its aftermath.

In several of the stories the reader is given a strong sense of the characters' powerlessness—lethargy or paralysis born of some deep fear, guilt, or despair. The narrator accosted by the unknown man from Prophets Street is forced by an inner compulsion to listen to the latter's accusations; the onlooker at the hanging of the village lad in wartime Ukraine watches passively, unable to intervene or even look away—"some strange force made me remain there until the end" ("Reflections Beside a Young Pine Tree"). In the disturbing story "The

Ice Floe," the first-person narrator is staying the night at a peasant woman's house in a Russian village while his wife gives birth in the local hospital. His reaction upon hearing what he thinks is the murder of the old woman in the night is to "[. . .] curl up. Keep silent. Bury your weary head in the fresh hay." In the morning he is paralyzed by a feeling of guilt and is torn between his need to go to see his newborn baby and his feeling of obligation to report the nighttime incident. Even when the events he thought he overheard are rationally explained, he still feels himself to be an ice floe, carried helplessly along by the rushing river, unable to act. In this he, like many of the other characters in the stories, is reminiscent of the helpless figures in Franz Kafka's prose. When Mann's protagonists *do* act, their actions often unleash disturbing forces or lead to tragic results: the frenzied attack on the cactus hedge by the narrator of "The Lizard," the obsessive pursuit of the SS man by the American soldier in "A Man in a Cloud of Dust," and the pogrom that results from the Jewish innkeeper's rebuff of the alcoholic Polish nobleman ("A Ruined Fair").

In *Seeds in the Desert* the breadth and depth of Mendel Mann as a writer can be discovered: he is Jewish but universal. His writing encompasses the particular existential traumas of Jews in the twentieth century and, at the same time, the moral issues all human beings face. He re-creates the atmosphere of real places with meticulous care for detail but at the same time evokes the mysterious forces that lurk beneath the surface of the land and the human psyche and threaten their stability and very existence. He depicts both the broad sweep of vast landscapes and the telling detail of a twisted smile or a trembling hand. Though set in the mid-twentieth century, his writing addresses timeless issues through the techniques of a modernist. As in much modernist fiction, there is seldom a feeling of absolute clarity of events or motivation in Mann's evocative narratives. The filtering of events and characters through the prism of the mysterious narrators' perception creates an atmosphere of veiled uncertainty and strangeness. The mood of Mann's stories brilliantly evokes the enigmas of the world.

– *Heather Valencia*

Seeds in the Desert

The Bedouin market in Beersheba is empty. The day is passing and shadows stretch out toward the desert horizon. A lingering camel contemplates the pale crescent of the moon. A truck leaves clouds of dust trailing behind it. There are vehicles laden with sacks, sheep with matted brown fleeces squeezed together, the braying of donkeys, and the dumb pain of trussed-up ewes with their black eyes and mouths full of laughing teeth.

I am searching for the young Bedouin woman who allowed the wind to lift the edge of her veil. I saw one large bright eye and one corner of her smiling mouth. She whispered something and I stood still. Just at that moment the noise of jazz drums boomed out of a radio. The café owner put out his wrought-iron tables on the pavement. The woman's dark veil fell over her face again, and I clearly saw the imprint of her lips on it. A few young lads came running up. One of them looked me up and down suspiciously.

I see the kneeling camel rising slowly to its feet.

These are the first days of the month of Adar. Here and there the sand is covered by delicate green shoots of vegetation, and desert plants bloom from under the scattered stones. But it is a short flourishing. One more week and that blessed green will disappear. First the distant landscape will turn a pinkish-yellow color, and then, when the first khamsin comes, the desert will be transformed into a coffee-colored carpet. By late Tammuz everything will look as if it were made of old tarnished silver. Then the winds will come and drive the withered bushes into the wadis, and the desert will be sown with seeds, so that by the month of Adar the delicate green plants can rise up once more.

I took my palm-wood walking stick.

"Hey, young man, are you waiting for someone?"

When I raised my eyes I saw a skinny old man wrapped in a cloak. He sat down slowly on the ground, put his trembling fingers to his face, and appeared to be shaking with laughter. But when I looked at him more closely, I realized it was not laughter but spasms that contorted the wrinkles on his face.

I must look really terrible, I thought, to have inspired pity in this old man. I looked at my dusty clothes and felt the stubble on my chin.

"Get up off the ground, old man. Sit down here at this café table."

I took him by the arm and sat him down beside me.

"Drink," I said.

With trembling hands he touched the edge of the glass of beer, peering at me. A pleasant coolness pervaded all my limbs.

"What drives you from your home, young man?"

I pointed to the green patches in the desert.

"At this time of year I can't find any peace. I have a kind of urge to flee from the empty desert within me and to see the flourishing, flowering desert spreading out before my eyes."

It was already dark. The gentle breeze carried the perfume of blossoming plants.

"That is the scent of hursinghar, the flower of sorrow," remarked the old man. "Would you like me to tell you a story that I heard from a beggar in Calcutta?"

"Calcutta?" I asked, noticing for the first time that the old man bore a resemblance to the immigrants from India.

"I am a Jew from India—from one of the tribes that returned . . ."

He carried on speaking for a long time, talking about the big markets full of Chinese silks, hand-woven materials, and all sorts of fruit—nutmegs, lemons, and olives.

"A young god descended to our Earth, and somewhere in a village of blossoming cherry trees he met the most beautiful young girl and had sexual intercourse with her. But then he regretted having sinned with a human creature. He was afraid that his kingdom would be inherited by a human being. So he consumed the girl with his fiery breath. She was transformed into a little heap of ash. It was as if lightning had burnt up a blossoming cherry tree. The girls from all the surrounding villages came to mourn her death, and her ashes were saturated with tears. One day a storm blew up, and the ash was dispersed by the wind. Wherever a tiny speck of ash fell, the ground became barren and salty . . ."

I felt the touch of the old man's warm hand, and the sound of his voice did me good.

The perfume of myrtle leaves and cinnamon arose from the flowering orchards, and when I closed my eyes I felt as if I were swaying along in a cart at night on the roads of Mazovia, traveling with my mother to the orchards we had leased . . .

It was late. I parted from the old man and wandered off around the streets of Beersheba. I tried in vain to shake off my waking dream, and a cloud of cobwebs seemed to engulf me. The dream I had that evening was of the reawakened steppe, of the woman's large eye appearing from behind the veil and the wind kissing her lips through the gauze. She was barefoot, and her arms smelled of sweat and donkey dung. The knuckles of her fingers were dark, the nails stained the color of peeled thorn-bush twigs.

Lying on my bed in the shabby little hotel in the Moroccan quarter of Beersheba, I find myself bursting into bitter, defiant laughter. I go and throw open the window. Again I hear the noise of the blaring radio. Now the tables are occupied by women with double chins, and in the gutters children are playing with abandoned cigar butts and poking about in the rubbish from the Bedouin market. Prams stand beside the café tables. Hookahs. A young mother has taken out her breast, round and white like a full moon, and she thrusts the nipple into the mouth of a crying baby. The sharp neon light falls on the tables. I stare at the mother's moon-breast with the tiny child sucking on it.

I am scared of the screams that will pierce the heart of the night like a knife. I know they will soon begin. I pray to almighty God that He will protect us. The silence also frightens me, for I constantly seem to hear sinister footsteps. "The flower of sorrow blossoms in the night," the old man had said. That must be the jasmine, whose flowers come out after dark. Through the open window I can smell the shashlik and falafel being fried under the night sky.

I am tired from having wandered around the whole day. Tomorrow I will leave here early in the morning, take my palm-wood walking stick, and set off for the small settlement a few miles to the south, where my friend Avner lives. Whereas I can never find peace of mind, he is the kind of person who is at home wherever he goes. If I leave before sunrise I will arrive in time to find him in his house. How long is it since we both arrived in Haifa on that Italian ship? Five whole years!

This happened a few days ago: the woman with full lips and silver rings laughed. "You once told me about the silver-green lichen, a plant with no roots, which the wind carries from tree to tree. It sucks the sap from the branches and the leaves, and it destroys the trees."

She looked me straight in the eye and said mockingly, "I didn't know that plants can behave like human beings . . ." It's only now that I understand the scorn in her laughter. Why did I not sense it immediately? Perhaps I was too blind with lust. Yes, there was some truth in her words—she wanted a home, and I had rejected her. I breathed in the soporific perfume of the flowers of sorrow. For years this woman had wandered with me along my life's desolate pathways. She had listened to me talk for hours on end, paying attention to the slightest blink of my eyes, and that had made me content. At least during those nights I felt I was not alone. How she watched over me! She accompanied me through all sorts of dangers and led me forth into life. I had felt certain of her until that sudden laughter. Her words were sober and sensible, and this reasonableness cut open my veins. I was contorted with grief, but all at once I shook it off like a tree shaking off the lichen fronds that attach themselves to its branches. And now I feel fine. I hear the cry of a camel in the distance. Down in the street the lamps are already extinguished. I can't get to sleep. From the next room I can hear muffled talk and the shuffling of feet on the floor. A door creaks as it swings open.

I drape my jacket around my shoulders and descend the dark stairs. The owner of the little hotel is sitting on the front doorstep smoking. I stop and think to myself, "What will I say to him as I go past?" Should I tell him that the shuffling around in the next room is preventing me from sleeping? After all, I like this noise, and even strain my ears to hear it. It is the silence that upsets me. I had seen them creeping in furtively, first the red-haired woman with her swaying hips. I had stared at her plump, bare arms. A pungent scent of fresh, hot pita bread and cheap perfume had wafted from her. Her companion had pressed against the wall and winked at me with a dull eye.

"There'll be a heat wave tomorrow," remarked the hotel owner.

He spoke in a hard, hoarse voice, but I was grateful to him for having broken the silence that had overwhelmed me. He waved away the spiral of smoke hanging around his face and looked at me with small, watery eyes. In the moonlight his face was pale and sickly yellow. I was sure he was now smoking his nightly dose of hashish, and breathing in his smoke, I had a feeling that these moments were different from all others and would remain in my memory forever. What had happened to make these moments on the hotel doorstep so distinct?

I sat down on the steps and closed my eyes. I felt a stubborn desire to breathe in the cigar smoke. I had the impression that I was somewhere in a strange land, standing beside a broad river, in which reflections of clouds were floating around. I strained my eyes to see the opposite bank, but I couldn't. A pleasant breeze from the river enveloped me . . .

My silence provoked the smoker to start speaking again. He stood up and muttered into the darkness of the desert: "A khamsin. Do you not feel the hot wind?"

I took my jacket off my shoulders, unbuttoned my shirt, and enjoyed the feeling of the warm wind on my chest.

"Where do you come from, stranger?"

"From the other side of the river."

"There aren't any rivers here," he said.

"There are. Just now I was standing on a shining river bank."

He smiled, turning up his eyes so that only the whites were visible. I wanted to smile with him, but all I could manage was a grimace.

Somewhere far away, across the ocean, I once saw forests devoured by a type of lichen that takes the form of clouds of fine silken threads that the wind carries from tree to tree. They hang on the branches like tattered rags, and they absorb all the sap from the tree until it dies. Only a few trees escape death when the strong winds shake off the silver-green strands of lichen, freeing them of these garments. I am now like one of those naked trees that has escaped its silky entanglement. I am content in my solitude, and yet I yearn for those times when I felt her clinging, silky caress.

"Give me something to smoke," I said.

The pupils of the man's eyes were visible again. He looked at me uneasily.

"I'll go and get some from the bar."

"Give me your cigar butt."

"No, I mustn't."

"Why not? Do you begrudge me it?" I suddenly started laughing. "Never mind, my friend of the night, we will wander off together like two brothers along the same paradise paths that the smoke conjures up for us. Take me with you to the land that rises up in the smoke, so beautiful and sad, and disappears along with the smoke. Ha ha ha!"

My laughter shocked him more than my ranting words.

"It happened a few days ago," I told the landlord, this stranger, without any idea why I was revealing my innermost self to him in the middle of the night. I simply felt the need to talk and couldn't restrain the flow of words. "I drove her away and then instantly regretted it. I was happy with her, although I knew that she was a closed book to me. Her past was like a deep, dark well. Her words were like the clinging, silky lichen threads. Now I am alone. I should have remained in harness like the foolish ass. Look what has become of me. I can't find any peace of mind. One should be able to exist in quiet contentment, to submit humbly to one's fate like the plants of the desert. How often they are buried by the blowing sand, and yet even from beneath the sand they push up fresh shoots. Their roots grow deeper and stronger."

It was as necessary for me to talk as it was to breathe in the night air.

"Come, I'll take you somewhere; it's only two streets away from here."

I followed him along a dark lane and into a little street flooded with moonlight. Only now did I realize that my companion was extremely tall, etiolated, and bent, with a hard, wrinkled face like a dried fig. His urgent whispering drew me on.

We stopped at a low house with bare walls. He knocked with one finger on the opaque windowpane. A head appeared, filling the whole window. I saw tousled hair and the whiteness of a nightdress. The door creaked. An old woman stood there and spoke very fast in Arabic. She held her loose nightdress together with both hands. In the little room a meager flame was burning.

"Come," he said. "We can go back home now."

I didn't ask him why he had taken me to that house in the middle of the night or what he had discussed with the old woman. But when we arrived back at the shabby hotel I heard hurrying footsteps, and when I turned my head I saw a young girl approaching. She stopped a few feet behind me.

"This is Zouhara."

"Zouhara?" I repeated.

"Yes, she's a prostitute," he said, giving me a friendly pat on the back. "Hey, Zouhara, come closer. This is the sad man . . ."

She surveyed me with a strange, mocking expression, muttered something, and then came closer with sensual, feline movements. This sudden switch from mocking to seductive sobered me. I turned away from her and locked the door of my room, shut the window, and lay down under my quilt. I heard their muffled words outside on the street, a loud, angry shout from Zouhara, and then silence.

The silence of the desert enveloped me, filling me with a strange regret, though I didn't know what about. I felt as though I were lying on a stone floor and someone was ordering me to unpick an amazingly beautiful carpet. I undid strand after strand, and each one was borne away by a dismal wind. I knew that as soon as I undid the last strand, everything would be over. It would be the end of all my dreams.

I spent half of the next day wandering around the little streets. I went to a barber and had my dark brown beard shaved off. Around midday I went off to the little settlement where my friend Avner lived. I strode along, swinging my palm-wood stick, avoiding the main road and taking instead the little byways; I enjoyed going through sandy fields, looking for traces of birds in the sand and avoiding stepping on the silvery-green and bluish-gray plants that come into bloom in the month of Adar. It is good to walk through a desert in bloom.

In the distance I caught sight of the water tower, a few faded, reddish roofs, and the green patches that were the meager orchards. The closer I came to the settlement, the more impoverished were the fields. The vegetation was withered, and the miserable earth looked as if it were covered with fine, rusty powder. I kept stopping to look at the fields, peering at the traces of tractor wheels that ran through them.

It was already dark when I reached Avner's house, where I was received with a warm welcome.

I drank the coffee Khamida brought me and immediately felt better. I listened to the crying of the baby in its cradle and felt more at ease with Khamida. I was filled with great warmth toward her, uncomplicated by any stirrings of desire.

"What's wrong with you?" she asked. "You look tired and ill."

From a cupboard she took out a pair of ironed khaki trousers and a white shirt and laid them beside me.

"Clean up and change your clothes. We're going to the communal dining room."

I suddenly felt a lump in my throat and tears in my eyes, and when Khamida bent over the cradle, I left the room. I was remembering those days in Jerusalem when Avner broke through the Arab blockade. There he met Khamida for the first time. He came with her to my shabby student room and we sat on my iron bedstead. "Do you think I'll be happy with this dark-haired girl from Aden?" he asked me.

"Yes!" I said. She was cowering at the door like a captured doe, unable to understand his words, as he spoke in Yiddish. But in my enthusiastic "Yes!" she sensed the love I had for Avner, and she came over to me, laid her head on my shoulder, and wept. "Why are you crying?" I asked her. "For joy, because Avner has such a good friend." They left, and I didn't see them for a couple of years. And now here I was visiting Avner and Khamida in their home.

The dining room was noisy. As soon as the remains of the food had been removed from the tables and the tin dishes cleared away, the benches were rearranged.

"Will you stay for the meeting?" Khamida asked me. This was, she informed me, the latest phase of an endless discussion to decide whether or not they should leave this area.

I didn't understand. "Leave it? You want to abandon it?"

"The earth is salty," said Avner. "Did you not see the miserable fields? The ground is full of salt. At first the plants germinate well, but then everything withers. It is pathetic to see these plants struggle, then fail to flourish."

"Have you only just discovered the salt?" I asked in astonishment.

"No, it was obvious from the first moment. But we hoped that this salty earth would be good to us, that by cultivating it we would be able to make it fertile."

He spoke very quietly so that I didn't hear everything he said. I had landed in the middle of a disturbed beehive, and I couldn't comprehend all the buzzing around me. I would have left the meeting to go and look again at the withered vegetation, but I was tired and wanted to be with other people.

So I sat there silently, a stranger, observing the uneasy villagers. They slowly gathered around the tables. The men's faces were
sad and their movements heavy. They took out packs of cigarettes
with knotted fingers. Their utterances were sparse and brief, delivered with lowered brows. Their words seemed to lie on the tables
like discarded crusts of heavy, dark bread. The desert had painted
their faces a dull brown color, marked out with dark veins and lighter
sun wrinkles around their eyes and at the corners of their mouths.
I looked slowly from table to table at their tousled hair, which the
sun had bleached from black to a brownish color, matted like sheep's
wool and as coarse as desert grasses.

The women had gathered in a corner. Some of them were knitting, and one looked obstinately out the window into the darkness.
Another sat with her large breasts resting on the table, her head in her
hands. Khamida was telling them something, and I had the feeling
she was talking about me, because the women kept looking toward
the table where I was sitting.

Someone pushed back his bench and stood up. The room became
quiet. A woman with knitting needles in her hands looked around
thoughtfully, trying to catch the eye of one of the men. A child was
swinging on the open door, and from the yard the braying of a donkey could be heard. From the expression of indifference on everyone's faces I could see that they all knew what the man at the head of
the table was going to say. There was a palpable sense of impatience. I
thought that if he just stood there silently in the lamplight, everyone
would feel gratitude toward him. But when he started speaking, there
was a whispering around the room like the wind rustling through a
field of dry grass.

His words smelled of salt, and when I covered my face with my
hand I could taste little salt crystals on my tongue.

"The top layer of earth is fertile," he began. "The plants grow
as if the earth had been enriched with good manure. Everything is
wonderfully green and healthy, and then suddenly it's cursed with
this rusty film. When I got down on my knees to examine the young

wheat, I discovered that first of all the little tips get infected—on the third day you can see little specks of yellow, and then gradually the whole field is covered with rust. Even the agronomist couldn't understand how this blight originates, but I've discovered the reason."

He took a piece of cloth from his pocket and unfolded it to reveal a withered plant with bits of root attached.

"They only examined the top layer of the soil," he continued, "but the salt has penetrated downward. When the roots of the wheat reach the salt layer, they die. You can taste the salt on them. Try it. Look how ruined the soil is. No amount of deep plowing is going to help—the salt doesn't get washed away by the rain; it just sinks deeper into the earth. The salt simply collects in this hard earth mixed with clay and stones. Friends!" he exclaimed, raising his voice. "This soil extends for dozens of miles around us, because either there was once a seabed here or else the mists and winds from the sea carried the salt to us. Either way, we need to move our settlement thirty miles farther on. Do you not feel how the salt has impregnated our whole bodies? We have been banished to a world of salt and have become men of salt. Our pleasure is mixed with the taste of salt, and even our speech and our breath are salty."

When he finished speaking a tumult broke out. Some men stood up and started shouting, and the women looked uneasy. I tried to understand what was being said, but I was without success. When things quieted down, Avner stood up.

"Anyone who wants to go, can. He doesn't need our blessing. Why should this man want everyone to follow his example? Because he knows he's a coward! If *one* soldier retreats, he's seen as a coward, a deserter. But if the whole brigade retreats, then that's all right. It's easier to give up if everyone else does too. He wants to conceal his own feebleness by getting us to join in. Are we to give up our homes, where our children were born? I, for one, will not leave. That's my final decision, and the greatest soil expert in the world will not convince me otherwise. In a place where children are being born, it must be possible to grow the wheat for their bread!"

The din increased. I saw Khamida take Avner's hand and speak to the worker, who had obviously been offended by his sharp words.

The herdsman suddenly appeared in the doorway. I recognized him immediately, because when I had arrived at the water tower he had shown me the way to Avner's house. He sat down beside me and I smelled the odor of cattle and milk, honey-sweet and acrid at the same time.

"Here's Yehuda!" exclaimed Avner. "Ask him. He'll tell you about the fields and pastures, where in fact the salt is extremely advantageous for the cattle. How can we abandon land like this? And what if, after a while, the new place should be polluted in some way? Will we wander off again? Are we to be nomads on our own land? The wheat fields *will* flourish! This soil will be good to us! We need to keep plowing it, and with each plowing it will get cleaner. This has been proven. The land will help us."

A young man with a small black mustache and rolled-up sleeves shouted out, "Thanks a lot, but I don't want your bread of mercy! I've no desire to be some kind of hero, wrestling against God's decision. I'll fight against the desert dwellers, but not against Heaven. You say that leaving is cowardice? Well, I think staying is cowardice. So what's to be done?"

The women joined in the discussion, but they spoke softly and no one heard them.

Not far from me sat a man dressed in city clothes, drumming his fingers nervously on the table.

"Why do you not speak?" Khamida asked him.

The man fumbled in his pockets and finally pulled out his spectacles, wiped them, and then tried in vain to put them on.

"It's your land, and you must decide . . ." he began.

A woman's voice interrupted him. "That's enough prevaricating! Just speak clearly: yes or no!"

The agronomist continued stammering, and I saw the mocking looks change into expressions of compassion toward this man from the Agricultural Center. Then I felt a hand on my arm. It was a worker's hand, and its owner's face was battered by the desert winds and dried up by the khamsin.

"What do you think, stranger?" he asked.

"You want me to tell you what I think?" I replied. "Have I the right to express an opinion about your land? To you I am just a stranger, a vagabond with a stick of palm wood, a wind blowing across the fields."

Then I remembered the words she had said before we parted. No, I said to myself. I am part of this earth, and its salt has formed me.

"Friends," I said, "if you don't mind, I would like to say something."

My voice seemed strange to me. Avner smiled and signaled that I should sit down and be silent. But it was strangely quiet in the room, and that stillness brought out my speech. My first words dispersed into a smoky fog.

"I am Avner's guest. I have a room in the city, but despite that, I have no home."

"Don't make excuses, just speak!" shouted my neighbor in a hoarse voice. "You've as much right to speak as him with the spectacles." Suddenly I was able to shake off my feeling of awkwardness. I stood up straight.

"One person spoke of leaving this land and another of remaining true to it, struggling with it, cultivating it until you get the upper hand. I say to you: don't go away. There isn't anywhere else to go! Here you have the salt to cope with, but in a new place there will be another problem. The salt of the earth is already circulating in your blood, and wherever you go you will have the taste of salt in your mouth. Life is full of grief, but you have been delivered from your grief by the salty earth. If you were cultivating good, fertile soil, you'd be sitting here after a day's work feeling exhausted, unhappy, and deflated. Who knows how many meaningless worries would be clogging up your life? Your life is stressful; your hours are completely filled with your determination to purify this soil. You should accept what God has given you to do; it is possible to live in a world of salt and still be happy . . ."

I heard stifled laughter and I exclaimed angrily: "I know people whose tears have permeated their skin, and they constantly taste the saltiness of these tears. Can they run away from their own face? Who says that life should be without any taste? Ease and leisure would corrupt you, and you'd become like passive, stupid sheep. You'd no longer be able to enjoy the taste of your coarse bread. You'd become the clay from which inanimate vessels are made. Accept God's Creation not with rebellion but with calm, quiet faith. That is man's destiny. You will not be able to cleanse your soil of the salt. That's an illusion. Whatever you do, in time the earth will return to the way it was on the seventh day of Creation. Let the grass grow as the Creator's hand planted it, and your sheep and cattle will multiply. If the fig tree withers, let it wither. Plant a date palm instead. I am sure God prefers the gracefully swaying shadows of date palms. Rather than battle against the earth, place your feet on it gently, with humility and love. Don't tear out its innards and pollute it with artificial chemicals; feed it with the dung from your cattle. Why has each of us adapted his life to the saltiness of our acrid days? How much humility do you show to those you meet? How often do your lips whisper words of false politeness? A yoke has been placed on your shoulders—why do you want to get rid of it?"

The silence had deepened. I heard someone breathing heavily. I paused, seeking Avner's eyes. "I have cast off my yoke. Has it made me happier? I have deserted my 'salty earth.' I tasted its bitter fruits. I took fright at its strangeness and the chasms I saw opening up in it. And what has become of me? I am a vagabond! I can find no peace. My days used to be filled with love, hatred, vexation, suspicion, jealousy, anger, and lust—they were the fullest days of my life. And now? I'm a defeated man. Nothing happens in my life, no one waits for me, I need nothing. My days pass by before they have really begun, and I cannot distinguish between one day and the next. They are like gray sheep wandering on mournful, fading twilight meadows."

Avner came up to me and took my arm. "Come. Your words make me so sad I feel like weeping."

But I couldn't stem my flood of words. The people started leaving, gloomy and dispirited. Two women approached me.

"I beg you, stay here," I said to them. "I will come and live among you. I will seek her out and say quietly to her, 'Come with me to the village among the salty fields, for the salt has already become part of our blood. There we will be happy. I was unkind to you, and for that I ask your pardon.'"

By the time I had finished talking, everyone was leaving the dining room, but Avner was waiting for me at the door. It was a starry night, and we walked arm in arm. Avner did not speak.

"Why are you so silent, my good friend?"

"What has become of you?"

It was not so much a question as an expression of pity and grief.

"Be strong!"

I took my arm from his.

"Why do you not pay attention to my simple words?" I said. "Each of us is a slave to foolish things, or to unworthy human beings, but it's God's Creation itself that you people here want to fight against. You submit to the serpent, but not to the earth. Bend down low before it, get on your knees, because the earth that tolerates you is holy. You swallow down all kinds of vile substances, you breathe in poisons, you plunge your arms into foulness, you entwine your bodies in filth and sweat, you let yourselves be enveloped in cigar smoke, in the dank air of wine cellars, in mold, in filthy refuse—but the salt of the earth, the crystalline salt that brings you healing, is not pleasing to you!"

Khamida was wringing her hands, and in her eyes I saw tears that I knew I had caused. She was sorry for me. Now I felt pity, not just for myself but for her too.

Why had I come here to inflict my anguish and my madness on them? Why had I upset their peaceful home? Why had I burst into this torrent of speech in front of the toilworn people of this desert village?

I wanted to calm Khamida, but I didn't know how. Perhaps I should remind her of our Jerusalem days? No, that would just deepen the wound. I could still remember the warmth in her eyes and feel her hot breath on my shoulder.

I stood by the cradle and looked at the sleeping child. What sweetness; what gentle breathing. Long, dark eyelashes, a little mouth with full lips that twitched as the little one dreamt of his mother's nipples. Tears came to my eyes, and I tried to hide them. I went to the window and said, "It's already late." Though Khamida could not see my tears, she sensed them in my voice.

"Drink a glass of milk," she said.

Avner showed me the iron bed and put out the light.

As soon as I closed my eyes all sorts of thoughts swam into my mind. Once again I saw her. This time she was beautifully dressed in a light frock with little blue flowers on it. She was going along a poor little lane, which I recognized as the one where I had walked with the sinister hotel owner from Beersheba. What is she doing here? In my dream I follow her, unnoticed, and see her stopping at a brick house. An old woman appears in the doorway, followed by the girl who had looked at me so mockingly. The old woman, the girl, and she, my beloved, are whispering together, and then suddenly all three turn toward me and burst into raucous laughter. I creep away along the wall. There's an old man beside me. "Who are you, old man?" I ask.

"Don't you recognize me? I am the Jew from Calcutta."

He leads me along. "Let's go to the fields over which are spread the ashes of the wonderful young girl who was seduced by a young god, then consumed by the divine fire of his breath." The old man leads me over fields and rocks, and we descend into valleys. A cloud floats overhead, and in it appears the young god, who then descends to the earth. He bends down on every hill and rock, gathering up the ashes of the beautiful girl he had consumed. For centuries he has descended from the heavens to collect her ashes in the vicinity of the shining Mount Hermon. Soon, when he has collected all the little flakes of ash, he will breathe life into them, and the girl will be re-created, even more beautiful than before. From the fragrance of the flowering meadows and the singing of the birds, I sense that she is about to appear again on our earth.

The old man whispers to me: "I must tell you that as soon as she rises from the ashes, this god, consumed by lust, will once again throw her down on the desert sand and burn her with his breath."

At dawn I left Avner's house, and I arrived at the outskirts of Beersheba when the sun stood high in the sky. I took my rucksack, which I had left in the hotel room, and waited for a jeep to take me back into the city.

I stared at the rusty wrought-iron café tables. A Bedouin passed by slowly, and in his shadow walked a young, barefoot girl. A donkey was tied to a dead tree stump. The radio was blaring out a melancholy desert song.

As the barefoot Bedouin girl passed me, a breeze lifted her veil, revealing her large, black, lustrous eyes and her lips, moist and full like ripe pomegranates. Her slender body swayed in time to the rhythm of the music. I followed her with my gaze. When she disappeared from view, my old sadness returned.

I open my arms wide, longing for someone to come to them. It doesn't matter whether it is the woman whose dark past scared me or the one who looked at me mockingly in the little back street at midnight. Perhaps it will be the Bedouin woman who will one night flee from her tent in the desert to the servant market in the little street where I live, and there I will meet her. I am ready for you all to come, for you are the salt of my good, sad earth.

The Old Jackal

Ali ben-Kardun sat in the shade of a cactus hedge. It was midday. An old jackal crept through the dying orchard like a shadow. What had driven this old jackal out of his lair in broad daylight? The sandy lane was empty now. No sign of human footsteps were to be seen in the sand. A night wind had blown away their last traces and had covered the sand with silvery pollen.

It was time to eat his meager meal. Ben-Kardun opened a basket woven from palm leaves and spread a small gray tablecloth over the prickly pear needles. The basket contained several little green bottles of homemade oils, remedies consisting of ground olive roots mixed with the blood of slaughtered eagles. He unrolled a little piece of linen and sniffed the dried mountain herbs from his distant village in Iraq, which was inhabited by Kurdish tribes. What would he do when his supply of herbs ran out? He raised his head and looked at the eastern horizon. No, from here he couldn't see the Judean hills; the dying orchard blocked out their distant peaks. From the hill where the mosque stood they could be clearly seen. And that was the place where these plants grew.

He put the palms of his hands together and said a blessing over the brown, cornmeal pita bread, pricked all over by the point of his knife; he had baked it early that morning on hot stones not far from his clay hut in the village of Sallama.

"What drove the old jackal from his lair in broad daylight?" he wondered again. "I know. A snake. A coppery brown, shimmering snake! He was dazzled by her smooth back gleaming in the sunlight, and it seemed to him that the day was pierced by the hiss of her venomous tongue. Ha ha!"

There was bitterness in ben-Kardun's laughter. His face, wrinkled like a shriveled fig, and his dried-up hands, with long fingers like the yellowed veins of palm leaves, seemed to join in the laughter. But when he bit into his bread and felt the stinging of the ripe prickly pear hairs on his tongue, he began cursing his own old gray head, a real donkey's head: "What sort of demon persuaded me to sit down under a prickly pear bush when the red fruits are ripe?" The slightest breath of wind blows the stinging silver hairs around in the air so that they hook on to your skin and get into your mouth; the stinging continues for days. Who persuaded him to take that wild Gamliela from the Kurdish village as a wife? It must have been the devil himself! Why did he bring her to this land, just so that she would desert him? A snake had attracted the old jackal. The snake was his wife, and he was the pathetic jackal.

Over there he knew all the Kurdish villages. He was an itinerant healer who had inherited his knowledge from his ancestors. He excised corns from people's feet, cured trachoma, and cooled the heat of chicken pox with ointments. As if by magic he was able to ease back pain, remove swelling from women's legs, and make varicose veins disappear. He had squandered a fortune on that snake.

How sure he had been that in his old age he would be able to live peacefully in the Holy Land. She would earn money from doing housework while he would sit comfortably in his little courtyard in the evenings, waiting for her. Sometimes he would go into town with a basket of vegetables from their small garden—and so he would live out the rest of his days according to God's commandments. Instead, his world had been turned upside down. One day when she came to collect her basket, she threw down her wedding dress of red cloth embroidered with gold thread and decorated with little silver coins. He did not understand what this meant, and he wondered if, God forbid, she had taken leave of her senses? It was only when a dark-haired young man appeared in the doorway, waiting menacingly for the slut to pick up her things, that the old man realized what was going on. "Are you her father, old man?" the young fellow asked in Hebrew, his voice full of mockery. Gamliela remained silent, with a stupid, stubborn air. She didn't even raise her eyes to look at him. "Get out! Get out!" Ali ben-Kardun screamed, shaking his fist at her.

On the third day after her departure he pulled from behind his iron bedstead a wooden box containing his medical instruments and herbs.

"I heal swollen legs, I cut out corns, and I can make your varicose veins disappear like magic . . ." Ben-Kardun wandered around the former Arab villages that spread out east of Tel Aviv as far as Lod and Ramla. His Hebrew was mixed with Arabic and Kurdish, and the women did not understand him until he opened his basket and showed them his ointments, his knife—so razor-sharp that it could cut out corns without any pain—and his fragrant balms. Then they gave him friendly smiles.

The courtyards were empty. In the little kitchens the women were busy at their paraffin stoves. They were good to him, bringing him drinks of cold water.

He couldn't communicate with the Ashkenazi women, though he particularly liked them. The day before, one of them had sat down on an old Arab sofa, raised her yellow, flowery dress to her knees, and shown him the knotted veins on her legs. With his long, bony fingers ben-Kardun had touched the swollen veins and run his crooked little finger along the hard skin below her ankles, murmuring to himself. Then he sat down on the floor and opened his case of ointments. As he was massaging her swollen veins, he kept stealing glances at her face. She had fixed her gaze on the dusty old cypress tree, but the secret pleasure she felt as he massaged her legs betrayed itself in her trembling lips. She had a broad backside, her heavy hips moved rhythmically, and the softness of her naked arm made him feel weak. Ali ben-Kardun smiled broadly and suddenly raised his head; the large teeth in his half-open mouth gleamed like a row of juicy dates. She smiled back at him.

She wasn't an Arab but a Jewish woman. If she were willing to marry him, he would lie at her feet for days on end. He would submit to her utterly, with the subservience he had drunk in with his mother's milk, for he had been raised among fierce, warlike Arab tribes. Had she a husband? He would find out that very day. Why had she invited him into her house? Other women covered their faces with dark veils; they called in female neighbors and would not allow him to treat them without one of their family being present.

Now ben-Kardun lingered by the cactus hedge. Perhaps he should wait one more day? It isn't good to be too hasty. He wanted to go back home, but against his will he found himself walking toward the woman's house. He recognized the footprints in the sand that he had made the day before. If she was alone in the courtyard it would be a sign that she did not have a husband. If an owl should hoot in broad daylight, that would be a sign that he should cross the threshold and greet her with "Shalom!" It would be a good omen. His steps became slower and slower. He was already at her wall. He could hear the hens clucking in her yard. Ten steps more. And suddenly he heard the muffled hoot of an owl. He knocked on the door in the wall: "Erm . . . just wanted to look in, ma'am . . . *lo yoter* . . . that's all . . . I just wanted to see if the ointment was working . . ." He laid both hands on his heart. "*Bli kesef* . . . no charge, I assure you. Ali ben-Kardun is an honest man, an *ish tov* . . ."

She was alone in the yard. Like a jackal's, his eyes peered into every corner. He breathed in deeply to see if he could smell the scent of some man who had been there before daybreak and had gone off to work. He couldn't discern evidence of anyone. She sat down once again on the sofa with the torn cover and protruding springs and uncovered her legs. He prostrated himself on the stone floor.

She spoke to him in a mixture of Yiddish and Hebrew, talked loudly, laughed—the submissiveness of this man lying at her feet soothed her heart even more than his fingers had soothed her swollen veins. From the other one she had never heard a kind word. That man had always been agitated and angry, and one day he went to stay with a girl in Jaffa, opening a bar there. A bar, was it? Ha ha! In reality he had taken up his old business again: it was a brothel—and the port is nearby. She laughed.

Suddenly she sprang up. Ben-Kardun was still sitting cross-legged on the floor. What was he stammering about? She looked him up and down with an expert eye and said, "Hey! Enough lying around doing nothing in this heat! Go and dig around the saplings in the orchard, clean out the henhouse, and see to the vegetable beds . . ."

As his glance fell on the hoe, he understood what she was saying.

She put away his basket of herbs and watched the old man striding boyishly toward the little orchard.

In the evening they sat together at the table and ate. He told her about the copper-brown shimmering snake gleaming in the sunlight, which had driven the old jackal out of his lair in broad daylight.

"Ha ha ha! God is good to His creatures. God is full of mercy. The old jackal has found a new lair in broad daylight . . ."

By the Ruins of Apollonia

From the old harbor in Jaffa to the place where the Yarkon falls into the sea is about three miles. I love walking along the shore in the cool of the evening. Sometimes I cross the bridge and wander as far as the ruins of Apollonia. To my left is the sea. At Jaffa it is green, but here in this desolate place the water is a muddy gray, and the sandy beach is covered with decaying brown vegetation, bits of wood, palm fronds, broken stones, and detritus from the city's sewers, all cast up by the waves. At Tel Aviv the coast is flat and sandy, and the water is colorless. Yellowish, foaming waves swell up, but as they approach the beach they become calm and gleam. It's only in winter that the sea surges up wildly, its waves the color of the loamy red earth of Sharon.

At the mouth of the river Yarkon the sea is crystal clear. Ribbons of light glitter on the horizon and little, peaceful islands float on its surface, shining silvery green as though covered with mirrors. On the left the sands slope upward into *kurkar* ridges, long ago carved and gouged by the wild buffeting of the waves. Half a mile before the ruins of Apollonia the cliffs rise out of the sea, stretching up their silver spines. The waves beat savagely against the red sandstone ridges at the water's edge, tearing out chunks and grinding them into dust that glitters in the foam.

A wadi has carved itself out between the rocks. In the winter, during the time of torrential rain, yellowish-red streams of water rage there. But at the moment it is dried out. Far off on the horizon, near the wadi, is the little Arab village—whitewashed houses around a mosque.

The ruins of Apollonia lie half buried at the edge of the sea. A rock shaped like the spread wings of an eagle with a sharp, gaping beak guards them. Stone walls, great carved blocks, watchtowers, the gates of the city, and the fortified ramparts with their embrasures— all lie piled up in one place, blocking the path. Lumps of moss-covered stone are scattered far out into the sea, looking at dusk like the last surviving warriors who fell before the victorious armies. Soon the ships of the vengeful foreign king will appear . . .

Until late in the night I sit in the little Café Yamiyah by the seashore in Tel Aviv. I am bored and melancholy. I feel a hot desert storm within me, and I envy the wanderer walking toward a mirage. For hours he sees it before his eyes, a tranquil, serene vision of green fields, quiet villages, and springs of water. My images are of ruined cities, of the ripped-out entrails of the earth, fires on the horizon, the gleaming silver of a wing flashing among the clouds, and a mighty mushroom cloud rising up to the seventh heaven.

I turn away from the sea and follow a beautiful Eastern woman with my eyes. It's Zouhara, the Jaffa prostitute. A ship has anchored not far from the harbor. The water is dark blue. "Waiter! Another coffee!" Clouds of golden butterflies are fluttering around the lamp. An old man is dozing at a table. A boy in a black shirt is whispering to the waiter. Withered oleanders with rusty leaves. Two women on the verge of old age, arm in arm, with bare, blue-veined arms. Despite the makeup that covers their faces, a network of little gleaming wrinkles is clearly visible. Little Yemenite servant girls teeter past in highheeled shoes. The smoke of shashlik mingles with the breath of the sea, which smells like seaweed, the municipal sewers, dead fish, and the lumps of clay that are lying around the Jaffa seashore.

My mirages have disappeared, thank God! Now I can be a normal human being again. I will go home and think about the Yarkon falling into the sea, about the ruins of Apollonia, and about the ship that is waiting at anchor till sunset to enter the harbor. In my dreams I will see Zouhara and pity her. Tomorrow I will wait for her, and when she passes by I will turn away my gaze.

I search in ancient books for a description of the settlement by the sea, south of Caesarea and once called Apollonia. I rummage around the libraries but only find a few lines about it. No one can tell me why the watchtowers and walls fell from the top of the high stony ridge down into the sea. No one can tell me why the gates lie broken and scattered and why the ruins are guarded by a mighty stone eagle with outstretched wings. I shall never find out why the stones of the fortress sprawl over the whole surface of the sea all the way to the horizon.

Once, at the wadi, not far from the Arab village, I met an old man who was poking around the thorn bushes and peering into the cracks in the rocks. His white-striped garment gleamed in the dusk, and the sound of a flute mingled with the twittering of birds and the distant sound of the waves.

"What are you looking for, old man?"

The flute music stopped and a face peered at me; it was shriveled like a fig leaf before the first rain of the season.

"I am searching for the black serpent with the silver back." He pointed to an open basket woven from willow branches. "The black serpent will be charmed by my flute. Its music subjugates him. I shall charm him into my basket. He hears the quietest note of my flute, even when he is dozens of miles away. I am sure that he is hurrying to me at this very moment. Obviously there are obstacles in his way. It's not like it used to be when everything here was wild. Now he has to slither along asphalt roads, through villages and gardens. It is a dangerous journey for him—that's why it's taking him so long."

Again the old man put his flute to his moist lips, and his fingers moved over the holes. It was like the noise of a spring rushing between rocks and the delightful singing of flocks of birds in the grass.

"For eight years I traveled around the markets in Jaffa, the squares of Lod, the courtyards of old Jerusalem, with my basket and my snake. I charmed her with my flute so that she stretched out her head, writhed in a graceful dance, and hissed comically with her venomous tongue. She coiled herself around my arms and neck and laid her head on my hairy chest. A few months ago I brought back a wife from the market. She had been wandering around the streets of Jaffa, barefoot and homeless. Unfortunately she brought bad luck, because three days later the snake wouldn't follow the sounds of my flute. She lay coiled up in the basket, hissing angrily. She wouldn't even touch the food I offered her. So I could no longer go to the markets and fairs. At first I thought she was ill. But on the third night I heard a terrible scream. My wife was lying on the bed, twisting in pain. The serpent had bitten her and disappeared. I went out to the doorstep and started playing my flute, but the sounds were mixed up with the screams of the woman. *I must get the snake back,* I thought; *she's my bread and butter.* And I went on playing until sunset. I searched all around my little garden and beside the fence, listened intently, and continued playing the flute. But she didn't come back. At dawn, when I returned to the room, my wife was lying there, dead.

"For half a day I wept for my snake and my wife. Now Mustafa has no livelihood. Mustafa will become a beggar, wandering around with an empty basket, stretching out his beggar's hands. I went to the village elder and told him of my misfortune, but he sent for the police, who took me away to the city. 'You have killed old Fatima, Zouhara's mother! You set the snake on her so that it would kill her.' I was in prison for a month. They allowed me to take the empty basket and my flute with me. Now I'm searching again for the black snake with the silver back. I'm an old fool, I know it. I didn't heed the words of my father, God rest his soul, who said that two snakes must not live under one roof . . ."

I didn't see Mustafa again that summer, but every time I came to the ruins of Apollonia at dusk I was astonished to hear the bewitching melody of a flute. Where was it coming from?

I was destined to meet the old man once more. He was carrying the basket over his arm and his flute was hidden in his bosom. Should

I ask him about the snake? No, there was no chance that she had come back, for his flute's melody was no longer pure. The notes were false ever since the night his music had got tangled up with Fatima's cries for help.

"Why have you been wandering the same paths for a whole year, young man?" he asked.

"I am bored and melancholy," I replied.

The old man's face seemed to get younger. He raised his eyebrows. "How can a human being be bored in the open, wide world?"

"My world is meaningless. I am the slave of mundane trivialities. I am tangled up in a spider's web. Every day I see the dusty fig trees and the asphalt roads, I wander along the seashore as far as the ruins of Apollonia, and when I arrive home I fall on my bed, exhausted, with burning visions springing up before my eyes. I am tired and haven't the strength to face them. Everything around me takes me back to those devastated homes. I prefer the ruins of Apollonia—and since the day I met you there, they have been bathed in the melody of your flute. Now even your flute has been desecrated, and I can only hear Fatima's cries."

He was angry with me for mentioning Fatima's name and was about to go away. "All misfortunes come from snakes."

Mustafa turned around, stretched out his arm toward Apollonia, and said, "The destruction of Apollonia came through a serpent." His face was twisted with contempt. His teeth had a hostile gleam, and his voice had become thin and sharp. "Apollonia was built three times. The third time it was destroyed because of a woman. Do you see that dark blue arm? That's the harbor of ancient Jaffa. If you stare for a long time at the horizon, you'll see the mast of a sunken ship out beyond the scattered rocks. Can you see the silvery remains of an old ship drifting about? No, it's not the ship that's shifting but the waves moving it. The ship was sunk generations ago."

"Yes, I can see all the things you've shown me."

"The third time the ruins were rebuilt, and the walls of Apollonia snaked along the rocky shore, a sheikh ruled this land. His brother ruled in Old Jaffa. Allah lighted a fire of hatred in their hearts in order to punish them for their sins. They almost went to war because some fishermen's boats had been sunk and a caravan of camels laden with merchandise had been seized. Their hatred smoldered for years. Then the wife of the sheikh of the rebuilt Apollonia disguised herself as a foreign traveler and went to the ruler of Jaffa to try and restore peace between the brothers. Instead the brothers' hearts burned with an even fiercer rage because the ruler of Jaffa fell in love with the marvelously beautiful stranger. She revealed her identity, and he secretly sent a servant to murder his brother. He killed him in his bed. The people said he had been murdered by his own wife because she had gone over to the enemy and had even lived there for a time in his harem. Out there, at the rock that looks like an eagle, she was stoned to death by her own people. The mast you see belonged to the brother's royal ship, which was approaching the shore, armed and ready for battle. At that moment Allah's anger was unleashed, and an earthquake brought down the walls and the watchtowers. The gates were smashed, and even the sea retreated from the shore and became a rocky plain. Jaffa too was destroyed, and it was not rebuilt for generations. But Apollonia was never rebuilt; the ruins have remained as they were until this very day. And God's rage has never been pacified. The sheikh's wife did wrong—she wanted to be the queen of two kingdoms. The Garden of Eden has been empty since God drove out Adam and Eve, and Apollonia has remained devastated ever since the earthquake. My own little clay house is also a ruin. My flute's melody has been ruined since that night with old Fatima. The enchanted black snake will never return."

One winter's day in Jaffa, Mustafa's trial took place. I found out about it and went to the courthouse. The judge explained to him that he was being accused of having set his snake on Fatima while she lay sleeping in his bed, so that she died of the venom. The prostitute Zouhara was sitting there with a lanky young man.

"I am not guilty, Your Honor. I didn't intend it; it was just because of my stupidity. I didn't realize that two snakes should not be kept under one roof . . ."

He was sentenced to six months in prison, not for murder, because his guilt could not be proved, but for keeping a venomous snake.

I watched a guard escort him out of the room. Mustafa recognized me, stopped by my side, took the flute out of his bosom, and gave it to me.

"Look after it until I come back. You can play it in the evening when you are sad. But take care not to charm any snakes."

The Search for the Nabateans

The small archaeological expedition pitched two tents about thirty miles southeast of Mitzpe Ramon. They had already been searching for traces of Nabatean settlements for two weeks: heaps of stones, shards of clay pots, traces of water channels, and cisterns for collecting rainwater. One such cistern was discovered in a hollow among stones covered with sand. At first they thought that this was an ancient well, but in fact it was a subterranean stone cistern. In winter the waters of the Mussa wadi branch out into a network of streams that flow powerfully throughout the Negev and fall into these cisterns, filling them to the brim with yellow, sandy water. When the basins are full they overflow, and the water continues on to another cistern until it reaches the Mediterranean.

In the evenings the most senior member of the expedition, Amnon Giladi, drew the arteries of the wadi on a map by the light of a carbide lamp, noting where his calculations indicated the Nabatean villages were situated. The cisterns didn't fill with water every winter; there had been years of drought. He even recognized the extinct wadis. As earthquakes had altered the surface of the land, the streams had sought new beds and the settlements had been destroyed by drought.

For three days a sandstorm had been blowing in the desert, and the members of the expedition sought refuge in their tents among the rocks. They covered their faces with transparent silk cloths, but it didn't help. The sand penetrated everywhere; it was in the very air they breathed. It stuck to their eyes and throats, and it burned with a dry heat on their lips, faces, and skin. They decided to wait until this desert wind ceased, and on the fourth day the weather changed. At sunset, when night began its swift descent, flocks of birds flew by so low that one could hear their cry. Their silver wings were glittering. "That's the end of the sandstorm," said Amnon. "The birds are a sign of calm weather." Around midnight the moon rose; it looked like the shriveled udder of a desert goat, the stars like the red-veined, glassy whites of the eyes of thirsty sheep.

It is an uncanny feeling to spend a night like this in the desert. The sand had penetrated their skin. It was difficult to speak. They were weak with exhaustion. This was the hour of those who wander through the desert, smuggling hashish from Jericho to Gaza. Soon their silhouettes would appear on the dark horizon; shadows would dance around the plain and vanish in the wadis.

Amnon Giladi dragged himself up and strode over to the jeep. The motor refused to start. There were five of them: three female students and an assistant of Amnon's, a young American who had come to visit relatives in Israel. He had already been a film actor, a director of a company, and a lecturer in a Boston university. For several months the idea of settling in the Negev had fascinated him. One of the female archaeology students had taken him to a lecture by Amnon Giladi. Someone from the agricultural department of the Jewish Agency proposed to Amnon that he expand his project with a view to finding a suitable location for a new settlement. It was hoped that this young man's father would finance the undertaking. The son sent long telegrams to New York, requesting money and the complete outfitting of a small expedition. He ordered film equipment, and he even decided to invite along a film actress who came from a distant town in Arizona and was a very experienced horse rider. And now, when the jeep's motor gave a rough cough and then fell silent again, the young American decided that the next day he would buy some horses from the Bedouin. He would make a film that would amaze everyone. He would fulfill all his dreams. Everything that he had not managed to achieve in America would come to fruition here. He would become a film star, buy land, build a settlement, and amaze his father with his business acumen. He would gain an entrée to the academic world. Together, he and Amnon would publish a book about the Nabatean settlements in the Negev. The book would be illustrated with maps, photos, and drawings of the wadis. It would be translated into various languages and be in the catalogs of all university libraries.

The jeep traveled over the dark desert. Its wheels jolted over stones, thorny vegetation, and mounds of sand. The three female students sat huddled together, softly humming a desert melody.

The kibbutz guard called out into the darkness. Somewhere in the distance two shots were fired. In the windows of a hut little flames danced, and from the sheep pen there was the warm smell of dung and a murmuring sound, as if a stream flowed nearby.

Amnon had first taken the American along out of the goodness of his heart, but it was soon clear that he knew much about archaeology and was able to withstand the heat of the Negev. Instead of "Nathaniel," the girls called him "Nate" or "Nathan." They all thought he would stay for two or three days and then quietly leave for his comfortable hotel in Tel Aviv. But in fact he coped well and surprised everybody. Tall, fair haired, with long arms, hairy, muscular legs, and a loping gait—and wearing a dirty green shirt—this was how Nathaniel appeared in Mitzpe Ramon the first time he waited to meet Amnon. In the course of the two weeks his skin had darkened, and the fair hair of his unshaven beard accentuated the tan of his face. Several times during the night Amnon awoke to see Nathaniel sitting in the middle of the desert, reading a holy book by the light of the moon.

There was no one in the kibbutz dining room. Insects buzzed around the light. The night watchman put down his rifle and sighed. The girls had gone off to wash. The shower stood in the middle of the courtyard, screened by palm mats, and the girls' voices floated over to Nathaniel. The water was warm instead of cold, for the pipes had been heated by the sun all day.

Nathaniel lay down in the sparse grass beside the dining room, his face turned toward the dark night sky. Suddenly, in his mind's

eye, he saw his grandfather's face. The Bronx. Fragmentary conversations in *mame-loshn*. A distant memory of relatives in Poland. Passenger tickets that arrived too late. Letters to which no one had replied.
He began to work out the names of his uncles, but he got confused,
trying in vain to pronounce the Yiddish names. He wanted to grab
hold of the thread of his origins, but it kept breaking like gossamer
in the wind. All this had been hidden away inside him; his father had
never been willing to talk about those relatives. Nathaniel knew that
a great-grandfather had escaped from Siberia—he had been mixed
up in some kind of "business." One of his grandfathers came to Jerusalem to die. A month ago Nathaniel had wandered around the old
cemetery; as he searched for the tomb of that grandfather, Reb Nosn
Shapiro, he felt that he had come here to trace his roots, and now he
had found them in the arid Negev.

Bright desert stars and the distant howl of a jackal. The laughter
of the three girls as they washed under the taps. One of them was a
slim girl with narrow shoulders and a beauty spot at her right temple. The previous day she had stuck together the fragments of a jug.
Her fingers were long, slender, and agile, and as she spoke she moved
them about like the conductor of an orchestra. The second girl was
tall and had a long neck like a deer. She wore her hair short, and
one black lock would fall over her eye in a question mark. The third,
a small girl with red hair, reminded him of the women of ancient
Egypt, whose faces he had seen in the drawings in the pyramids.

All these impressions got jumbled together in Nathaniel's wildly
racing thoughts: his grandfather, his parents' reluctant words about
the relatives who had perished, his fight with a Puerto Rican who
had called him "Jew boy," and his nights in the Sixth Army during
the attack on Germany. He suddenly remembered the emaciated face
of a concentration camp victim and the ship in which he himself had
traveled here, packed with immigrants he'd seen from his first-class
cabin. He thought about the Nabateans, about the battles with the
Arabs in the Sinai, about the night watchman who had sat down with
his rifle between his knees. Was he still sitting there in the communal
dining room? Why was Amnon Giladi so silent? Was he, Nathaniel, as

superficial as they all believed? He smiled as he asked himself this question. *They don't know,* he thought, *that I am playing the role of a frivolous American tourist. This fits their preconceptions about American youth.* Why should he disabuse them? They would not believe him in any case. Once more he heard one of the girls laughing. Then he listened to the night.

The water had cooled down, and his body came to life. He knew he would not find rest on such a night. He thought he saw a shadow flitting across the ground to the stables. He walked out into the desert, convinced that the girl who had stuck the pot together would emerge. He waited for her; all his other thoughts and memories had faded away, and he felt an urgent desire to see her.

She would appear. He listened for her footsteps. It would happen before the stars were extinguished.

The Dove of Nablus

At first Abu ben-Salim was unwilling to answer the judge's questions. He stood with his head bowed. His pitch-black hair was unkempt, his long arms stood out from his sides, his ears were fiery red, and his dark, checked shirt hung out of his trousers.

Whispers reached him from all around the courtroom like the rustling of the wind over low grasses.

"Why did you leave Nablus? Who helped you cross the border? Where did you get the false papers?"

"Your Honor, I am not from Nablus . . . the papers are genuine . . . I am a Moroccan Jew, Yehuda ben-Tov. That is my name, I swear it on my life."

On the front bench sat a red-haired young woman with a child in her arms. A white shawl with a long silk fringe was draped around her shoulders.

She stood up hastily. One breast was uncovered, and the baby began to cry.

"What do you want from my Yehuda? Set him free . . ."

The child's wailing was thin and penetrating. The mother's dark-red nipple was swollen, and her breast moved.

The judge put his head in his hands and said something to the court clerk.

The clerk, a man with a spotty face that looked as if it had been hammered out of rusty tin, went up to the woman, covered her breast with the shawl, and said, "Come along. You are disturbing the court. You will have to wait outside."

Abu ben-Salim became agitated, and his hands sought a support. He looked at the clerk with contempt, then at the policeman standing beside him, and then he pulled open his shirt with trembling hands, revealing his tattooed chest. The judge peered at the dove with an olive branch in its beak and at the primitive lines in dark blue that were supposed to represent the Flood.

"Don't throw her out, Your Honor. I will tell the truth, and I want Tamar to hear it. Feed the baby, Tamar; don't be embarrassed. We all drank milk from our mother's breast. Let the baby be pacified."

The rustling in the courtroom grew louder, and the benches scraped on the floor—then it became so quiet that you could hear the windowpanes trembling and the breathing of the baby as it sucked.

"My real name is Abu ben-Salim. I do come from Nablus."

"You are an Arab?"

"Yes, Your Honor—an Arab, the son of an Arab."

Tamar wiped at her tears as they trickled down her breast onto the baby's lips.

"I have deceived Tamar and lied to everyone. But one thing I said is the truth: I will die at her feet. I will never forsake her. I will be a father to our child."

The judge interrupted him.

"Why did you leave Nablus?"

"It was fate—ordained from above."

"Where are your parents?"

"I only have an old mother. She was born in Ramla. Once, about a year ago, in a bar I overheard an Arab telling a few old men a story about a fortune he had hidden in a courtyard in Ramla, buried among the roots of a date palm. I listened carefully as he described the yard, the appearance of the tree, and the jar full of gold coins. I wanted to get some money, a lot of money, to buy a wife and a little bit of land and start a family. It was time. So I went to Ramla. I was drawn to my mother's town. The house where she was born would surely still be standing. I had heard so many stories from her about

Ramla, about the grand markets, about the camels decorated with embroidered cloths and the graves of my ancestors. I slipped across the border, avoiding various settlements and sleeping overnight in orchards. For two weeks I worked for a farmer, and I arrived at Ramla a couple of days later. I found the house and saw the date palm in the yard, exactly as he had described it. But how was I to get my hands on the treasure, since there were people living there and the yard was locked? Through the little gate I saw the inhabitants. It was the house of Tamar's parents. I didn't understand their language. I decided that I would creep through the fence at night and attack the roots of the date palm. Near the fence I found a mattock on a dung heap, and I spent half a day strengthening it and sharpening it on a stone.

"A light was burning in one of the rooms until late at night. I crept up to it on tiptoe and peered in. That was the first time I saw Tamar. She was reading a book.

"The earth around the date palm was hard, and I struck thick roots. Several times the mattock jolted against underground stones and rang out. A dog started barking, and a pack of jackals suddenly began to howl. The door scraped open and a strip of light fell on the ground, reaching the date palm. Tamar was standing on the doorstep. She wore the same white shawl around her shoulders. I hid behind the tree trunk and watched her walking to the cowshed; the cow's scent filled my nostrils. There was a smell of milk, and I heard water running from a tap. I left.

"The next morning I knocked at the gate, and Tamar's father came out. I said to him in Arabic: 'I am a good Arab. I will help you clear your garden of thorns. I won't charge you much.' When he didn't understand me, I showed him my mattock and my hands. 'No,' he said, closing the gate in my face.

"For a month I worked in an orchard. Then I bought two sheep and drove them to the gate of Tamar's house. 'Buy these!' I said. They asked me who I was. 'A Jew from Morocco,' I replied. 'I bought the sheep, but now I am in need of money.' And so we became friendly, and I started working for Tamar's parents. I made a stall for the sheep, repaired the house, and helped to lay tiles in the rooms. I also dug all around the date palm, saying that I wanted to plant flowers around the tree to make it look attractive."

The judge listened intently to ben-Salim's words. He raised his hand several times to signal that ben-Salim should stop talking, but the latter was unable to contain himself. He was speaking Arabic jumbled up with Yiddish words, but when he came to the description of the first night he spent with Tamar, he fell silent and his ears burned fiery red. "Your Honor," he said quietly, "after that night I left her parents' house. I intended to go back to Nablus. I realized that the Arab in the bar had deceived me. He was a drunk who borrowed money from everyone, promising that he would pay them back tenfold, as he had a treasure trove in Ramla. In a month's time, in two months' time, he said, he would definitely go back to get it.... He owed everyone money, and he even gave out signed receipts that promised he would pay them back with huge amounts of interest from his fortune in Ramla.

"I started working for the odd day, then spending a couple of days wandering around the city's Arab streets. No one asked me who I was. I enjoyed going to the cinema and spending time with the Jewish lads from Morocco.

"One day Tamar found me. In tears, she said to me: 'I'm expecting a baby, and it's yours. What are we to do?' 'All right,' I said. 'I'll stay. I'll not leave Ramla.'

"Your Honor!" exclaimed Abu ben-Salim. "That is the honest truth. What difference does it make to you whether I am Abu ben-Salim or Yehuda ben-Tov? I swear by my child, and by Allah, that I am an honest man, a just man. I'm not Jewish, but is that a sin?"

"It is a sin to lie. You did not give your real name. You have no papers. You crossed the border illegally. Maybe there were other transgressions in Nablus? Perhaps you've even committed a crime there?"

Helpless with rage and despair, ben-Salim tore at his shirt. Now the tattoo was clearly visible: a rough sea with a tiny ship sinking helplessly beneath the waves. At the same time a dove with an olive branch in its beak soared away, above the stormy sea.

All the people in the courtroom stared at his naked chest. Even Tamar looked at it with astonishment, as if she were seeing for the very first time the little ship among the waves, and the dove with the olive branch flying above the ocean.

The Lizard

"How did it begin?"

He had a pleasant, quiet voice. A white coat. Dark glasses, translucent though rather fogged, and long restless fingers that tapped the white table as if they were playing piano keys. But why is it so quiet? Why do I not hear the notes?

"You are a fine pianist."

The man in white suddenly stood up and asked uneasily, "You can hear someone playing the piano?"

"It was a large lizard, poised on the gray, crumbling stone wall. Its mouth was wide open. Its lower jaw and belly were making strange movements. The lizard's color and the texture of its scales were like a crusted-over wound."

"You're not answering my questions," said the man in white to the young man with dark, tousled hair and thick eyebrows that met in the middle.

"No, I don't hear anyone playing the piano. Your finger movements made me think of it. I don't know why I said that."

"Why did you tell me about the lizard?"

"I can't forget it."

The young man was sitting in a leather armchair. His hands were on his knees, his shoulders hunched, his hollow temples crisscrossed by fine blue veins that stood out, throbbing. His pale lips were split and his jaw jutted out, fiery red.

"Your name is Victor?"

The young man put his head in his hands and stared at the floor's flagstones.

"There's nothing wrong with me. I feel perfectly healthy. I don't know why I have come to see you. All I am asking for is a remedy for insomnia. Do you know what insomnia is like, Doctor? The long nights listening to the jackals howling and the secret night voices of birds as snakes coil around the tree trunks to reach their nests. The dying orange groves mixed up with the desolate sounds of bombardment. In my division we called them 'lowing oxen.'"

"You were at the front?"

"Yes."

"Wounded?"

"It healed twelve years ago."

"Show me the scar."

Victor stood up and unbuttoned his shirt. His hollow, hairy chest rose and fell rhythmically. The doctor touched the dark-bluish scars with two fingers. They formed the shape of a lizard with a wide-open mouth, its two front claws fastened on to the chest.

Victor began speaking softly: "The khamsin lasted for a whole week. The hot wind came in waves from the south. The cacti lost their smooth, bright appearance and shriveled till they looked like the outstretched hands of beggars. Fine pollen, burning hot and biting, settled on your eyelashes, stuck in your throat, and made every mouthful of bread taste bitter. The smell of dryness reminded you of ruins, of extinguished bonfires and stones that had cracked open. Your nostrils burned as if you had inhaled fire."

"Come on, speak!" the doctor urged. It was almost a command.

"On the first day of the khamsin I jumped up from my bed at daybreak. To the north the cactus hedge stretched out. It had turned a silvery green color, with ugly, misshapen heads. Often in the night I had heard among the prickly pears the hissing of a snake and the terrified cries of a turtledove. Desperate for air, I had opened the little top window of my room, which faced north. Even the palm fronds were motionless. Only the thorn bushes moved. The breeze seemed to be drifting along at ground level, but the prickly pear cactus hedge blocked its path. I suddenly had the idea of hacking down that cactus barrier. So as soon as day began to break, I took out the ax and sharpened it. I made sure the wooden handle was secure, and I tested the steel blade. The whetstone rang out in the dawn and echoed back at me like the distant, confused pealing of bells. Could that be the fire bell? Perhaps the eucalyptus forest of Mikveh-Israel was burning? Perhaps the thorn bushes of the mountains of Judah had caught fire. No, Mikveh wasn't burning. It was still enveloped in the foggy breath of the khamsin. The light shining from the mountains of Judah was coming from the rising sun.

"The cactus hedge stood in the shade. Thousands of heads bristling with sharp silver needles, and stems of dull copper with lighter strips and rings. Arms outstretched and petrified, as if after a blaze. A hydra with a thousand heads. I was determined to hack it down! The ax cut easily into the flesh of the prickly pear stems, and a yellow fluid covered its steel blade. This yellow stuff disgusted me. I felt a strength surging up inside me that I could not rein in. Pieces of the hedge were falling around me, and I didn't even hear their sound because the sharp needles pierced the dry earth as they landed. The silence made me even more agitated. Each time I struck with the ax, my grunts shattered the silence. From time to time, when it was awkward to get at the main stems, I used the mattock. Sometimes pieces of cactus fell on me, gouging my flesh and causing a savage, searing pain that felt like a poisoned arrow or the sting of a wild bee.

"By the time the sun had risen, part of the cactus hedge was already lying on the ground. My face was covered with yellow dust, my throat was burning, and my eyelashes were sticking together. I wiped them with my hands. Streams of sticky sweat ran down my back and chest. I couldn't breathe or swallow. A few times I left the cactus hedge and stood by the stone well. I stared down into its cool, dark depths and felt a strange sense of relief, accompanied by dizziness. I clung to the stonework of the well, as I felt the earth slipping away under my feet.

"At lunchtime I was hardly able to swallow down a bit of bread.

A feverish impatience drove me on so that I could not remain still, and before I had managed to finish my meal I was again sharpening my ax and rushing back to the devastated hedge. I was convinced that the cool breeze from the north would be able to pass through as soon as the hedge lay at my feet. The cool, fresh breeze would fan me, and I would be freed from some oppressive thing that was weighing me down. My garden would be enlarged by ten feet, there would no longer be sharp little hairs of the prickly pear fruit floating around in the air, and it would be the end of the lizards whose skin looked like a mass of wounds.

"By the time the sun began to set, the hedge was completely cut down. Now I used the mattock to clear the ground and take all the cactus to the wadi. I knew that each leaf would plant itself in the earth and put down roots, so that even in the wadi the cactus would not die. Years later there would be a cactus thicket there. Not even the wild torrents that rush through in the wintertime would be able to wash away the prickly pear plants. The debris of roots and thorns would be gathered up in the stream and carried out to the sea.

"I made dozens of trips to the wadi and back, attaching myself to a rope and dragging the chunks of the dug-out hedge through the wilderness of the neighboring gardens. In the evening I fell, exhausted, onto the mat of palm fronds on my room's earthen floor, and I lay there motionless, staring at nothing. But for a long time I was unable to rest; some force that I couldn't explain kept driving me outside into the yard.

"The heat had not let up, and it seemed to me that my feebleness came from my vain attempt to rest within the four walls of my little room. The terrible thirstiness of the earth made me sad. Suddenly I realized why my garden yielded such a meager harvest. The ground sloped downward, and the water, instead of being absorbed, ran off toward the wadi. I took my spade and decided to level off just one yard of earth, no more. The hard earth resisted my efforts. Again it rang out as if my spade had struck copper, and I listened to see if an echo would come. God's evening world was still. My temples were throbbing as if someone were pressing a tight, prickly crown of thorns onto my head. I started working by the light of the foggy moon of the khamsin. I must level the garden; I must smooth out the bumps so that the ground will be as level as a tabletop. Then in the winter the water will remain and the earth will be saturated. Then the streams will not carry away the fertile layer of earth and the manure that I spread on it every spring and autumn.

"My exhaustion brought a kind of release to me because it freed me from the pressure in my temples. All I felt was the pain in my joints, and this sensation calmed me down.

"I worked through the night. From time to time shadows slid past my feet, and I knew they were the venomous snakes that had lived in the cactus hedge. I lunged at them with my spade, but I didn't manage to hit any. Once, I heard the short, plaintive hoot of an owl, and our eyes met. It was sitting on a branch directly above my head, so close that I saw the reflection of my eyes in its huge black pupils. I was seized by a sudden panic. I wanted to scream, but I had no breath. I stumbled forward, falling several times . . . no, I deliberately hurled myself onto the ground and tore up lumps of earth with my hands, trying to crumble them and flatten them out. *Why am I lying in the middle of the field?* I wondered in amazement.

"I noticed that it was getting light. The beginning of a new day. A fever had entered me, and my breath was burning hot. When my glance fell on the stone wall, I saw the big lizard sitting there. Its mouth was wide open, and its lower jaw made strange movements.

"I don't know what happened after that. I found myself lying in my bed, with old Azariah, the wild-fig gatherer, sitting beside me, giving me a healing infusion of fruit, a cool, sweet drink. I begged Azariah: 'Knock down the stone wall! Destroy it!' My neighbor Fridova came by, wringing her hands: 'Oh dear, that's what happens when a man lives alone!' She looked at me coquettishly, wanting me to notice her garishly made-up face, her cleavage, and her knees, which she had bared as she sat down on my bed.

"Doctor, there is nothing wrong with me. I just don't want to see the lizard on the stone wall any more."

It was strangely quiet in the doctor's office. The doctor's fingers once again traced the scar on Victor's chest.

"You say it has been healed for twelve years?" asked the doctor.

Victor nodded and tried to smile. But his forced smile filled the whole room with sadness.

The doctor stood by the window for a long time, watching Victor walk away. His steps were unsteady at first, but then he started walking with a firm and regular stride along the deserted, sunny street.

The Mosaic of Ashkelon

At Ashkelon the sea is silvery green. At dawn, its phosphorescent veins shimmer with the mysterious light emanating from its depths, and the stone columns rising up from the shore resemble arms stretched out to distant oceans.

I have taken off my shoes and am walking along barefoot. It is good to feel the coolness of the early morning seashore. From the north comes a mild breeze fragrant with the scent of blossoming orchards. Probably from Sharon. Where are the sails of the little fishing boats? They would now be filled by this little dawn breeze, and their whiteness would harmonize so beautifully with the clarity of God's bright dawn.

About three miles south of Ashkelon the Gaza Strip begins. The fishermen are scared to set out at night for the southern shores because an unexpected wind can carry their boats on toward the Arab lookout posts. The latter are always lying in wait for winds blowing southward.

I was tired of the marble columns, the battered blocks of stone, the ancient wells with their thousand-year-old, twisted stems of olives and sycamores, and the statues whose faces are worn away to a blank smoothness. For hours I gazed at the folds of their stone garments, at their breasts visible beneath petrified drapery, and at the ornamented capitals of the columns. I dug around in the clayey soil full of pottery fragments, and it seemed to me as if those shards had been brought from the potter's workshop only the day before and scattered in the fields to make a barrier against the spring and winter floods; they were used to line trenches that were then filled with water to irrigate the gardens.

Now I am alone on the seashore at dawn. The world has turned its face from me. The distance is veiled in mist. Danger lies in wait to the south, and from the north there is no longer the scent of blossoming orchards. The pitiless sun rises higher in the sky, and the mysterious light from the sea's depths is no more than a fantasy of mine. The only truth is the fear that lurks here. Soon something sharp and dark will flash on the horizon. Could it be a spy ship from the other side?

I am standing on the shore, leaning my back against the rocks. Above me rise the towering columns, some of which are of marble and some made of a dark brown metal, perhaps bronze. Once upon a time they protected the harbor. How many generations have passed since then? The sea level sank until its sands were revealed in front of the rocks. I am now standing where, twenty generations ago, there was an abyss. We are living in an abyss, I said to myself, and I began to look around that rocky shore for a path so that I might clamber up to where the ancient gardens of Ashkelon once stood.

He suddenly appeared before me like a shadow and looked at me with a calm gaze, his eyes fixed and impassive. His face was dark, like old silver that had just been hammered out anew. His hair fell in large tangled black curls. His open shirt was damp and of a dull green color, as if woven from filaments of seaweed. Even the disheveled hair on his chest resembled the green moss on stones under the sea.

"Sir, you haven't seen a sailing boat with phosphorescent green sails?" he asked me.

"No."

He put both hands to his forehead, shading his eyes, and stared out at the distant sea. His fingers were long, with gleaming white joints. I was surprised by the grace of his movements.

"It looks as if the boat won't come today either," he said, as if talking to himself. "Ha ha, you mustn't lose patience, it will come.

I've already been waiting a thousand years. . . . What's a thousand years, after all? Look at the stones; they remember the days of Creation . . ."

He laughed, and his laughter cheered me up. I admired his agility as he jumped from one jagged rock to another, and I was amazed by his strange beauty. It was good to meet this young fisherman in the early morning, and to hear his laughter.

I didn't go to the ancient gardens of Ashkelon. They are desolate, and for two thousand years the stone troughs have been dying for the cool streams of well water. The basins have been covered by a salty deposit from the sea. The wild grasses with large, withered, starlike flowers are covered by dead snails with mother-of-pearl shells, which look like the eyes of desert birds that have died of thirst. What attracted me instead was the silence of the sea's mirror.

I will cast my line again; perhaps this time I will manage to catch a fish. I made a loop where the sharp hook was fastened to the lead weight. Then I found a round stone the size of three fingers and attached it to the line, tightening the loop round it, and hurled it far out into the sea. The surface of the water was broken by silver rings that spread out all the way to my feet. I moved forward into the sea. The line was suddenly pulled so strongly that it cut into my fingers. At the same moment a dark sailing boat appeared to the south.

From the shore came a shout. It was the same strange young man. He sprang swiftly down the winding, rocky paths, and some moments later I saw his fragmented shadow on the churning waters near the shore.

"Do you see the sail?"

Not waiting for my answer, he called out, clapping his hands.

"They're coming! Soon they'll reach the silver-green strip of water, and then it will happen."

My line had slackened, and I left the water and sat down on the sand. These fish are teasing me today. Every time I throw my line, I feel a large fish pulling the hook, but as soon as I try to wind the line around my arm, the fish disappears.

"What will happen?" I asked.

"Ha ha, I see that you are a stranger here. This is your first time in old Ashkelon. You don't even know the fish from our waters. Just now there was one instant when it was yours—at that moment you could have pulled in the line, and now there'd be a gleaming silver fish weighing perhaps five kilos twitching on the beach. But you let that moment pass. You couldn't distinguish it from all the other moments."

Suddenly he stopped speaking and his lips trembled. The disheveled, mossy hair on his chest seemed to fade. The boy sat down on the damp sand, rested his hands on his knees, and stared out in front of him.

In the evening, on the little streets of old Ashkelon, he accosted me.

"The boat will come tomorrow. Before sunrise. Will you be on the shore?"

"No."

"If you are, you will catch a rare fish. Sir, if you buy me a glass of arrack, I'll tell you a secret."

He whispered the words in my ear. The shashlik seller, her large, red hands with their scarlet-painted fingernails bloodied by the pieces of raw meat, winked at me. She put her finger to her temple and twisted it, then burst out laughing.

We went into a bar with a ceiling so low that our heads almost touched it. Several men stood bent over a low table. I could only see the spread fingers of their hands and the little yellow dominoes they had thrown down. One tall individual peered at me with a mocking expression and nudged the others with his drooping shoulder. They turned around to look at me for an instant and smiled through the smoky fog enveloping them.

"Hey, Salim, your little sailing boat hasn't arrived yet?" asked the man with the drooping shoulder.

"Your name is Salim?" I asked. "Do you want some arrack? Okay, I'll order some. Hey, Khavadzha!" I called out like a regular. "Two arracks!"

Salim sniffed his glass and then drank.

"You've heard of the cave that was discovered last year?" he asked.

"I had already been going there for years and admiring the mosaic by the light of a tallow candle. Once I remained for the whole winter.

"It started like this. She arrived by boat on the same day the Arabs ran away from there, when it became a Jewish state. I didn't flee with the Arabs. Why not? Because my mother was a Jewish woman from Safed. It was an unhappy love affair with an Arab that brought her here. Salim is my name. I stayed here alone in old Ashkelon when the men of the Haganah arrived. I said to them, 'My mother was Jewish, so I am Jewish.' They gave me bread and wine. At night they left the town.

"'We'll be back in the morning,' the leader told me. I was the only living soul there; everyone else had fled to Beersheba. During the night I went down to the sea. When I passed the place where the columns and the ancient sculptures stand, their actual faces emerged out of the stone. I heard a voice coming from one of the columns: 'We have revealed our faces to you because you are the sole heir of our fame and greatness. For thousands of years we have turned our faces away from the sinful people, but now we can reveal them. Look at us!'

"I fell to my knees. The pillars were flooded with mysterious moonlight. And then I heard footsteps. By the shore lay a sailing boat that looked luminous green. Then she came toward me and said, 'Salim, it's good that you have come to meet me. We have to get there in time, before the moonlight fades.' That's what she said to me. For an hour I walked beside her in silence. There was a boulder standing where a tamarisk tree grew. She bent down and touched the stone, and it rolled away all by itself. Then I saw a cave. A bright light streamed from it. 'Come!' I wanted to close my eyes but couldn't. The mosaic was shining. I saw the planets rotating, and around them moved the virgin, naked as the day she was born. Her body was bedecked with rings and pearls, and her long tresses cascaded down, gleaming with a golden light."

Salim fell silent. He picked up the glass of arrack and emptied it in one gulp. His fingers touched my arm, and I felt the heat emanating from them. He seemed now to be totally distant, seeing only the virgin with her naked body. His face was damp, droplets of sweat had broken out on his brow, and his hot breath made his lips glisten.

"Salim, what part of your story have you gotten to now?" asked the landlord. "Are you at the bit where she leads you to the tamarisk and the stone rolls away from the cave mouth all by itself? Or have you got as far as the cascading tresses? Ha ha ha!"

A few of the customers burst into thunderous roars of laughter.

Salim jumped up, flecks of foam gathering on his lips. He beat his chest with clenched fists.

"I will never darken your door again!" he said to the innkeeper. "I'm not going to bring in any more strangers to buy me arrack. You are always making fun of me. You're desecrating the truth. Just tell me: Who was it that led the archaeologist into the cave a year ago? Tell me! Jews! Admit the injustice you're doing to me! By all that's holy, answer me. You must answer me!"

With one shove he overturned the table. The dominoes all scattered on the floor and lay there with their black dots facing upward. Someone said to me, "It's true that Salim drew attention to the cave. There the mosaic was found, as well as some ancient wine jars and a beaker made of gopher wood."

"Tell me," Salim said, "how did I know about the cave? How? Did an angel from heaven reveal the secret to me? No! It was *her*. At dawn I accompanied her back to the boat. I watched her float away from me. 'Guard the cave. I shall come back the same way, but remember, Salim, you must stay as honest and pure as you are. Only do good deeds, and then I shall appear again. It will happen soon. But you must be there to welcome me. Wait for me by the old harbor.'

"You are unbelievers, sinners," he continued. "All the ancient stone faces revealed themselves to *me*, whereas they have concealed themselves from you, deep inside their stony intestines. . . . Only lying and baseness have domination over you, and you are preventing her return. You . . ."

Salim's fists unclenched. He put his hands together as if he were praying and quietly left the bar. He didn't even look at me. I sat for a long time over my glass of arrack, listening to the dominoes falling on the low table and to the hoarse conversations in Hebrew and in Arabic.

Around midnight a girl appeared in the open doorway of the bar and looked me up and down. "Taltila, here's someone who's waiting to hear the end of Salim's story!" called out the landlord.

She came up to me, touched the little tiled table with one finger, and turned on her high heels in order, it seemed, that I should see her ample thighs and legs.

"Sir, you want to hear the end of Salim's story? Come with me and I'll tell it to you. Come, it's not far from here . . ."

The sea was restless. On the rocky shore I can see Salim's silhouette. Far away, on the horizon, there is some kind of dark shape. Could it be the little sailing boat?

With My Own Hands

One evening ten years ago, a man stopped me on the beach in Tel Aviv and said, "Sir, I know who you are . . . forgive me for addressing you. Night is approaching fast—the sunset passes so quickly here, before one looks around it's already dark. But I must speak to you, for today something happened to me."

"Who are you?" I asked. "What's happened to you?"

"Will you hear me out? Have you got enough patience?"

"Yes," I said, imagining that I was in for a convoluted story with a long-winded introduction, lots of unimportant details, and confusing digressions. Before me stood an elderly man with graying hair, wearing an open-necked white shirt. His forehead was furrowed and his eyebrows lowered.

"I can speak on one condition: you are not to write about this now. On no account must you write it down, nor even relate it to anyone. Give me your hand and promise me this."

I had the urge to walk away, but somehow I couldn't. The sharp tone of his words, his demanding gaze, and his outstretched hand held me in their sway.

"Ten years from now you may write and speak about our conversation, but not until then. Not even a day sooner. And even then, you must not mention any names, nor the place where the event occurred."

I held out my hand and felt the stranger's trembling fingers.

"Today there is a khamsin blowing," I said, in order to break the silence. "It's a stifling wind, but here on the seashore it's not so unbearably hot."

I would have continued talking about the khamsin and the stifling heat if he hadn't interrupted me, almost angrily: "Please listen to me."

We were facing the bay of Jaffa. The stranger looked at the sea and began.

"On the eighteenth of January, 1944, I entered a little town on the Horyn River with the Soviet army. Once, more than three thousand Jews lived there. Once? This 'once' was only two or three years before we entered the town. Now there were only ruins. Bearded Ukrainians with piercing eyes shuffled along the walls of the houses. I was a young officer. One night we caught a group of Ukrainians in the forest— Ukrainians who had murdered Jews, Russians, and Poles. They refused to surrender their weapons. Those same people who had collaborated with the Germans had been turned into fighters for an independent Ukraine. My goal was to find out what role they had played. We granted amnesty to those who were innocent or who agreed to collaborate with the Red Army. We had been informed by an old Ukrainian woman that one of them had murdered a whole Jewish family not far from the mill. He had shot the Jews who were in hiding—a father, a mother, and several children—with his own hands.

"Death sentence! That was what I demanded of the garrison commander, and he confirmed my verdict. I decided I would carry it out. Why, you will ask, why did I volunteer? Because I wanted to. I felt that we, too, had to take revenge with our own hands.

"At daybreak I heard hammering as they erected a gallows for three Gestapo collaborators. Suddenly there was a soft, tentative knock at my door. The soldier on guard duty stood there and reported to me that there was a woman waiting, holding a parcel and eager to speak to me. But it was still so early. Should he let her in?"

The stranger paused and asked me: "Do you have a cigarette?"

"No," I answered, "I don't smoke."

"I beg your pardon," he said. "Neither do I. I don't know why it suddenly entered my head to ask you for a cigarette. Perhaps because at a similar point during the war I had asked a soldier for one. I still smoked back then. You see how easily one can be transported back in time and forget where one is? I really do have the urge to smoke . . ."

"Come. We can buy cigarettes nearby."

But he did not move. I realized that asking me for a cigarette was an unconscious way of pausing to catch his breath, because it was so difficult for him to talk about this.

"The woman was young, and she was carrying an infant in her arms. She wore a short sheepskin jacket, her head covered by a dark woolen shawl. I instinctively felt that she was Jewish, and without waiting for her to speak I said in Yiddish: 'Sit down and warm yourself by the stove. Are you from the shtetl?'

"She didn't speak but just shook her head, undoing her scarf. Her lovely face was illuminated by the fire in the stove. Suddenly she burst into tears, and even the little baby sobbed. I took the child from her, laid it on my pillow, and called one of the guards. 'Put on the samovar and bring some milk for the child!' I said. 'It's not necessary,' said the woman in Yiddish. 'I have everything that I need at the moment. I have come here to implore you not to kill the father of this child.'

"I gave a start. 'Kill the father of this child? What on earth makes you say that? I would be happy to meet another Jew. What's wrong with you—do you have a fever? Your face is flushed, and your eyes are full of tears. Where is your husband? Where is he? Of course I will help him.'

"'He is not my husband. He is the father of my child.'

"'Bring him to me immediately. I'll see what we can do for him.'

"'He can't come. He has been arrested. He'll soon be hanging from the gallows.'

"I jumped up as if I had been bitten by a snake and banged on the table.

"'Get out! I don't want to see you anymore. How dare you come here to plead for a murderer!'

"She picked up the child, wrapped it in the shawl, and moved toward the door. I barred her way.

"'Who is the father of your child? Tell me his name!'

"'Umaniuk.'

"'Nothing can save him from the gallows,' I exclaimed angrily. 'There are witnesses to testify that he murdered a whole Jewish family by the mill. He tricked them into leaving their hiding place. There weren't even any Nazis around when he murdered them. He did it with his own hands. After that he took part in other brutal acts.'

"'I know what happened in the hiding place by the mill. I was there. He shot everyone except for me. My father, mother, sister, and brothers . . . he spared me, the eldest of the children . . . and after that he took me as his wife. I lived in his house. . . . He is the father of my child. My parents would have died anyway; he told me that the Germans were on their tracks, that they would torture everyone and drive them naked into the pits—there'd be no escape. Their only escape was to die. . . . And after the child was born, he was good to it. I'm so unhappy . . . I'm only eighteen . . . I just want to die . . .'

"Involuntarily, I stroked the baby's little hands and found that I was trembling.

"'Don't hang him. Put him in prison, but don't hang him.'

"I opened the door and waved her away. I poured a glass of tea, but without drinking it I went out into the street.

"It was a frosty morning. The gallows with its three nooses stood ready, and the truck holding the three condemned men had arrived. They were wild fellows with the faces of bandits who had been hiding out in the forest. Three assassins who had begun their barbaric career by murdering Jews and then, when there were no Jews left to kill, had murdered Poles, and then after that had shot their own countrymen, Ukrainians, because they refused to give up their last sheep. The first to be led to the noose was Umaniuk. I peered into his face, trying to find some resemblance to the child, but there was none. I was pleased about this. 'I want to put the noose round his neck,' I said to the person in charge.

"When I touched his neck I felt as if I had touched a slippery snake. The truck moved off and Umaniuk dangled in the air, and at that moment I heard a strangled sobbing from the woman. She was standing by a corner of a ruined building, holding the child in her arms.

"'Come,' I said, taking her hand. 'I am driving to Rovno tonight and will take you with me. There are Jews living there, whereas here you are all alone.'

"After a moment or two of silence, I continued: 'Don't be angry because I shouted at you this morning. I beg your pardon for that. But what happened to Umaniuk had to happen.'

"We traveled to Rovno in silence. The short journey of forty kilometers took us more than two hours. We were shot at several times by Umaniuk's accomplices, who were still at large. I gave her money and told her to look after the child—which, as its mother, she would certainly do in any case—but I wanted to make her understand that I felt a closeness to this baby, and it was innocent, like all children. After that I didn't see the woman and her child again.

"At least, not until a short time ago, when we met in Jaffa in one of the little alleyways. A woman stopped me: 'Excuse me, you look very familiar.' Yes, it was her. 'Your baby must be a young man now?' I said. The woman whispered agitatedly: 'Oh, God, you are the young Jewish man, the Russian officer from that shtetl in Volhynia?'"

The elderly man stopped speaking. Night had already fallen. A dark ship was passing on the horizon. Its siren would soon blare out. Jaffa was illuminated by hundreds of lights, but they didn't reach down to the seashore. I assumed the man had finished telling me this sad story, and I hastily reached out both hands to him and was about to move away.

"One moment; I have something more to say to you . . ."

I stared at him. All I could see were shadows passing across his face.

"I was in Jaffa today—I was invited to the bar mitzvah of that boy. His mother has a husband. She referred to me as her 'relative.' I was in the synagogue and witnessed the boy being called up to the Torah. There were two people weeping in the synagogue: his mother and I. I, who had hanged the man who had been his father with my own hands. I too was called up to the Torah, but I couldn't say the blessing—my throat was choked. I had been wandering along the seashore for hours when you came toward me. I simply had to tell you; now I feel a sense of relief. Look at these hands of mine. On that long ago day they slipped the noose over his head and I felt the joy of vengeance. Do you think it is possible to take revenge? Oh, how the blood of the victim and the killer is mingled together! I am sure that now, if you shake my hand, a shudder will go through you."

The man went away. I met him a few times after that in the streets of Tel Aviv, but he never stopped, just nodded his head and hurried past.

It's now ten years since that evening. I am sitting in a café in Paris, looking at the people whose faces are so bright and happy. It is summer. Along the avenues the chestnut trees are in blossom. Yes, this evening ten years will have passed since the man told me his sad tale.

He said to me then: "In ten years' time you may write and speak about it, not before." I have kept my promise to him.

All around me people are drinking coffee, and I sit here, hastily writing these lines. I write them with pain, with sadness, and with a glittering tear in my eye.

The Encounter in Ramat Gan

"Excuse me . . ." I said. "I think I know you . . . we've met somewhere before . . ." She looked at me with an air of curiosity that quickly changed to suspicion.

"Avivele, come!" she said to the little girl who had been hiding behind her mother's big blue shopping bag.

It was a hot morning in the month of Tammuz in Ramat Gan, at the hour when mothers take their children to kindergarten, doing their shopping on the way back.

She was a dark-haired woman in her late thirties with heavy eyebrows and, around her temples, fine wrinkles that looked like rays of light radiating from her dark eyes. She walked away without responding. I felt guilty and wanted to remedy my error, so instead of looking after her I hastily turned my back and opened my morning paper.

Today my bus was late. I stood leaning on the bus shelter, leafing through my newspaper. I remembered her face very well—I wasn't mistaken. Or was I? No. I *had* met her, about ten years ago. I had been taking this bus every morning for two years now, and she must live near here, so why had I not encountered her before? The khamsin is going to blow today. The coolness of the night still lingers in the air. What's the news in the paper? I realized that I had no idea what was in the newspaper. Just big, screaming words. I had been standing there for half an hour, staring at them without taking them in. I crumpled up the newspaper and stuffed it into my pocket.

The unknown woman was coming back from the kindergarten. Avivele was already playing with the other children. The heavy shopping bag weighed down one of her shoulders. She had the early morning freshness of an oleander in full bloom. I laughed at myself. No, I simply had to give her an explanation, so that she didn't think I was the sort of man who would rudely accost an unknown woman in the street.

"Please don't be offended at my speaking to you again. I wouldn't have done so if you hadn't just been passing by while I'm still waiting for my bus. I do know you."

I said these words with an urgency and certainty that even surprised me. She put her shopping bag down on the pavement and looked at me silently.

"I traveled across Ukraine with the Soviet army, and somewhere in a shtetl in Volhynia I met you. It was a strange encounter. Don't you remember the Russian soldier who talked to you in Yiddish? Have you forgotten a night journey in a truck with two armed soldiers?"

She wrung her hands and her lips began to tremble. "I don't know you. I don't want to know you!" she shouted. Her vehemence made me certain that she was the woman I remembered.

At last the bus came. I was grateful to the driver for saving me.

The whole day I thought about what had happened that night in the shtetl in Volhynia. I really didn't want to remember it. What sort of stupid curiosity had driven me to address that woman? Why did I have to remind her of those days? No, it wasn't just curiosity. It was absurd vanity, a subconscious desire to remind her of my noble deeds. If I had done some good then, I was destroying it now. Not just destroying it but trampling a human being underfoot with my soldier's boots—a human being who had managed to escape from a swamp and reach the shore.

The next morning I met her again at the bus stop. She was wearing dark clothes, and I didn't see the blue shopping bag. She looked as if she was heading into town, and I wondered if we would be taking the same bus. I didn't greet her, but she came up to me and said: "I've been waiting for you for an hour. I didn't know exactly when you would be traveling. I have to speak to you. Perhaps I was a bit harsh yesterday, but that wasn't my fault—it was yours. Come!" she ordered me.

I followed her. She led me through several little alleys. On the small balconies people were beating rugs and hanging out clothes. The milk sellers were already returning with empty cans. She walked in front of me, and when I tried to catch up she increased her pace.

We went into a municipal park. Her silence was making me uneasy. I felt that something was going to happen, and I was starting to feel afraid of her.

She suddenly stopped, and I saw that her face was fiery red.

"Erase that night in Volhynia from your memory. The woman you met then is dead. She doesn't exist anymore. Another woman lives in her place—not far from here, in her own villa with a garden. Her husband is a civil engineer. She has two children, a six-year-old girl and a three-year-old boy. It's not just the children who were born here—*I* was reborn, raised from the dead. Why have you shown up? What do you want from me? Remember, we don't know each other; we have never met. It is a horrible mirage."

"Yes, it was surreal: a dream that you and I both dreamed simultaneously. Forgive me," I said. "I have really made a mistake: it wasn't you."

Despite myself I smiled at her. I wanted to show her that I didn't take the incident too seriously, but apparently my smile came across as sarcastic because she became angry. I had the feeling that she despised me.

"But you don't want that woman you met to be dead. That would destroy the legend of your great achievement. You want to revive my shame for the sake of your pathetic egoism, just so you can pat yourself on the back. I despise you. You have come to call in a debt. I'm sure you would have liked me to respond to you with warm, humble, grateful words, to invite you into my home, introduce you to my husband and say to him, 'This is an old friend I met in those difficult times.' You would have kissed my children, bowed politely as you left, and been happy and proud of your behavior . . .

wait, don't walk away. Don't be a coward. Have the courage to hear me out."

She sat down on the uncomfortable bench made of eucalyptus branches. She had calmed down, and her face was no longer burning but pale. Her upper lip was damp with little drops of sweat.

"When you met me I was twenty years old. I had been hiding in the woods among peasants for three years. A Ukrainian had raped me in the forest and left me lying in the snow. He returned at night with bread and warm milk and took me to his home. I lived with him until he was murdered. A comrade of his shot him. 'You'll be *my* lover now,' said the comrade. '*He* is lying by the pond in the forest.' I wept. I was eighteen years old. 'Take me to the pond,' I demanded. We walked through the night under bright stars and a full moon. Yes, it was Apanasyev lying there. Although he had mistreated me, I loved him. Hritsko said to me: 'I will save you, Jewess,' and he threw me down onto the cold forest floor, not far from my dead lover's body. I lived hidden away in his house. He threw a party every Sunday, and I had to come and sing for them, and I began to sleep with his comrades from the forest. I had to; they forced me.

"Then Hritsko disappeared, and I was left completely alone. When the first Soviet divisions arrived, I ran out into the village street shouting, 'Take me away from here! Save me! I am Jewish!' A Russian officer took me to a little shtetl and installed me in a comfortable dwelling. The next night he came with lots of food and vodka. He left at dawn. His name was Volodya. I didn't see him again. Instead, he sent someone with a note from around Rovno. They say his grave is beside the river Horyn. Then his comrades started coming to see me. They were always drunk, and I started drinking as well. Then they began to turn up one at a time. 'How did you manage to survive?' one of them asked me. I laughed drunkenly. 'You slept with Germans, and with Ukrainian bandits.'

"I wept, I screamed, I laughed. 'It's all the same to me,' I said.

"Then a young Russian officer appeared, his lips pressed together, a lock of his black hair falling over his left temple. He spoke to me in Yiddish, and when I heard the sound of the language I wanted to weep. But I had no tears left. He didn't want to drink with me, and he left.

"In the middle of the night a truck drove up and two Russian soldiers entered the house. I heard their heavy footsteps on the porch and saw the dazzling light of their lanterns.

"'Citizen, get dressed. Come with us—you're under arrest.'

"I stood there in my nightdress, screaming, 'Why?' But it didn't help. They gave me ten minutes. They were stern and silent. I sat in the open trailer of the truck between the two soldiers. We traveled for an hour, and I recognized that we were on the road to Rovno. I knew then that they weren't going to kill me. If they had been bandits in disguise, they would have shot me immediately. I don't know why, but as we approached Rovno, when I saw the first little houses of the suburbs, I started to sob. Perhaps it was the memory of my childhood and of my parents, who had perished in the town.

"The truck stopped; the driver's door opened swiftly and a soldier jumped onto the back platform. The two other soldiers stood at attention. I immediately recognized him in the gray of the dawn—it was the young officer who had spoken to me in Yiddish.

"'Don't be scared. Nothing bad will happen to you. You are free. We'll find a place where you can live among Jews. In Rovno there are some thirty Jewish families. I'll bring you to an elderly Jewish woman, and you can live with her. Remember, if you come back to the shtetl and lead the kind of life you were leading, you are done for. Stay here, and later, when it is possible, you can go on to somewhere else, along with other Jews.'

"I lay there curled up and didn't say a single word. I was thinking: *Let them do what they want with me. It's all the same to me.*

"I had an iron bedstead in a miserable, half-ruined house that I shared with another woman. From time to time they brought me money and food. I knew that it was sent by the black-haired officer who had spoken to me in Yiddish. And now you have turned up. I know that it's you. Tell me, why have you suddenly reappeared out of the forgotten past? Is it sheer curiosity? Is it perhaps . . . no. I don't know why. Go away—be well. . . . Everything I have told you was invented, a lie, a mistake. My life has started now, here, in my home, with my husband and children. Forget, and let me forget."

She went away and did not even look back.

I said to myself: "All this was a mirage, a daydream in Ramat Gan. It is an unhappy invention. It is not true."

Swarthy Meylekh and the Turtledove of Sharon

Swarthy Meylekh had wandered around Jaffa for a time, not knowing what to do with himself. Should he become a porter in the harbor? Help the fishermen? Or perhaps work in a big yard full of scrap iron? He had been in Ramla for a week, then in Lod, and now he had come back to Jaffa. During the nights he slept opposite the clock tower in a vegetable shop that belonged to someone from his hometown. He hated the sea, the smells of the seashore, the motorboats, the patches of oil on the water, the voices of the porters, the noise of the trucks, and the baking-hot cement walls. The big scrap metal yard belonging to Mr. Artsiali made him feel sad and downcast: rust, tar canisters, skeletons of old machines, and a small, rotund man who immediately called him by the familiar *du*.

Swarthy Meylekh was born in a shtetl in Mazovia, and he was drawn to flat, open pastures. As a boy he had roamed over all the roads and pathways with the horse traders. Now his dark, curly hair had turned grayish brown, like grass at the edge of a road after a fire has scorched it.

His acquaintance with the Yemenite, Yussuf Tsalakh Gamliali, had brought him both good luck and bad luck. Thanks to Yussuf he was able to settle on a piece of land not far from Abu Kabir and get himself a wife—but thanks to him, too, Meylekh had fallen afoul of the police and suffered the humiliation of being arrested and taken before the judge.

It had begun one evening when Meylekh was unloading the scrap iron from Yussuf's cart; he was surprised to hear the Yemenite quarreling with Mr. Artsiali in Yiddish that was spiced with familiar curses and contained plenty of genuine Slavic words. From that moment on he began to warm to Yussuf Tsalakh. He patted Yussuf's horse, stroked its neck, and laid his heavy hand in a friendly way on the wagoner's shoulder. Then they sat together in a bar drinking glasses of arrack, and Meylekh poured out his heart to Yussuf. It did him good to talk to someone who had been born in this land. He felt he was talking to a close friend, and with this conversation he was forging a relationship with this new land, with the strange town of Jaffa, its inhabitants, and with the animals. Even the Yiddish language, though sprinkled with Hebrew and Arabic words, sounded natural in Yussuf's mouth. This was the only language Meylekh could speak—and he talked quietly and hoarsely, his voice breaking with grief and despair.

"You see these hands of mine? They can harness horses and tame the wildest of bulls. When I saw your horse I was overcome with nostalgia for the days when I drove horses like that from Płońsk to Danzig. I'm going to die bit by bit among all that scrap iron. I have absolutely no one to talk to; they are all Bulgarians, Turks, and Arabs, and my countrymen, the Polish Jews, have moved to Tel Aviv and don't want to have anything more to do with swarthy Meylekh. On the ship, a servant girl called Zelda swore to me that we would set up house together and live like decent people, but she ran off the week after we arrived here. A young man from the camps who had come to Jaffa before us started a bakery, and she left me for the baker. She's living with him now. I sleep in a dark little shop and have to leave with my straw mattress before daybreak. Do you see what has become of me? I've become a vagabond! And to cap it all off, I have no language. I am a dumb animal."

Yussuf Tsalakh saw that the young man was wiping away tears. Their eyes met, and Meylekh seemed ashamed of his weakness. He jumped up and burst out into strange, unnatural laughter. He jangled the remaining coins in his pocket and refused to let the Yemenite pay for the last bottle of arrack that they had shared. He was drunk, and when they reached the corner of the street he was seized by a sudden burst of emotion and cried out, "Swarthy Meylekh will again become what he once was! It's not the end of the world! I will harness horses again and have my own wife and children!"

Far from lasting very long, his triumphant mood disappeared as swiftly and unexpectedly as it had come. The Yemenite took the young man to the darkened shop, but it was already closed up with several iron bars.

"Leave me here, Yussuf; I can sleep on the steps. It's a warm night."

Meylekh stared at the bright stars, and it occurred to him that he was not yet more than forty years old—he was still a young horse driver, and time had no power over him. He had to start afresh! To stride forward again!

The next morning both of them left for Abu Kabir, which is not far from Jaffa. Yussuf showed him a deserted, ruined Arab house.

"Make a door with a padlock and shutters for it, and it will be yours. In this country, one just helps oneself. The Arabs have fled, so don't wait—no one will come and chase you away. Fence off a piece of land before someone else does it."

Later that day the Yemenite brought in his wagon, Meylekh's iron bedstead, and the straw mattress he had used in the vegetable shop.

For several weeks Meylekh lived in terror that someone would come any minute to throw him out. It occurred to him that perhaps this small, constantly smiling man, this Yussuf Tsalakh, was playing a joke on him. Swarthy Meylekh was afraid of the men with leather briefcases, and of the police officers who regularly stopped not far from his clay hut. One day, however, his fear disappeared when two workmen came along and said to him that soon they would be installing a water pipe in his yard. And it was at that time, when the well-watered plots began to green up around the dwelling in Abu Kabir, that Yussuf Tsalakh came along and outlined his plan.

"Meylekh, my brother, listen to what Yussuf Tsalakh Gamliali has to say to you. Listen carefully, because I'm telling you that without a wife you are not going to achieve anything, and in this country it's not so easy to find a wife. A wife is like a turtledove from the fields of Sharon. You have to entice her into your courtyard, and then she will become tame and stay with you. About three miles from here in the village of Moldet lives a distant relative of mine, Obadiah Zarai, together with his daughter. And although he is my relative, I tell you frankly that he is a bastard, a real son of a bitch, which has led to his daughter being left on the shelf, with the prospect of dying an old maid. He has power over her because he has a ready fist. Now he's in a tight spot. His horse has fallen, and the stones that press his olives aren't turning anymore. Yesterday he was in Jaffa looking for a horse, so I will get a horse from an Arab, and you will take it to Obadiah. When he asks you the price, you shouldn't answer immediately; tell him that you are letting him have the horse for a few days. You'll manage this with your Yiddish because he understands your language a little, and if he doesn't understand everything he can call the neighbor. After three days you should tell him that you have your own property in Abu Kabir and that you need a wife. Say to him, 'Give me your daughter and I won't ask any money for the horse. A fair exchange.'"

Swarthy Meylekh could not comprehend this extraordinary proposal. Something about it seemed suspicious. How could Yussuf be giving him the horse for nothing? And how could he suggest such an "exchange"?

Before he could ask any questions the Yemenite preempted them.

"Don't worry about the horse. We'll soon get it back from that bastard Obadiah—you can rely on my comrades. I know that what I am suggesting is a trick, but the result will be honorable. Zahara, his daughter, will be your wife, and she won't have to slave anymore for that old man and remain an old maid to the end of her days."

Yussuf Tsalakh had a score to settle in this matter. Years ago he'd had a love affair with Obadiah's daughter, and they often used to meet in a dark little room belonging to Hassan Salim, who owned the bar at the port of Jaffa. Yussuf had to endure so much trouble from Obadiah that eventually he had enough. Or perhaps it was the fault of the red-haired Ashkenazi girl who threw herself at him with such ardor that he abandoned his first love? From that time on he had no peace of mind; he was to blame that she never married, for after that she disliked going to town and became even more subservient to her father. Because Meylekh was a peaceable fellow, Yussuf felt that the time had come for him to atone for his sin before God.

Peaceful, happy days followed for Swarthy Meylekh. He had a little plot of land and a wife, the daughter of the man whom Yussuf, his brother, had called a son of a bitch. His wedding had taken place in the village of Moldet under a sycamore tree, and Yussuf and his friends had accompanied him to the wedding canopy. But he wasn't destined to have peace and quiet for long because exactly four weeks later a policeman appeared and took Meylekh away to be questioned by a magistrate. What Meylekh could not forgive or forget till his dying day was the shame of being led away in handcuffs.

"Swarthy Meylekh! You have stolen a horse from Mohammed al-Zahari in Jaffa and have sold it to Obadiah Zarai, resident in the village of Moldet!" the magistrate said in Yiddish. "Do you confess to this?"

Meylekh wiped the sweat from his face. He looked around with suspicion and anger, but the fact that the magistrate had spoken Yiddish to him, even though he couldn't understand all the words, gave him courage. He took a step toward the magistrate and declared, "I am not a thief. I am a horse driver, as were all my ancestors. Like them all, I have always been an honest man and will remain so until my dying day. In Jaffa I heard that Obadiah had a daughter whom he would allow to get married if one gave him a horse in exchange for her. I brought him a horse, didn't ask any money for it, and left the horse with him. I visited them often, and he himself suggested the exchange to me. That was what I wanted!"

He wanted to continue speaking, but the magistrate interrupted him. "Where did you get the horse?"

Meylekh was disconcerted. "Where did I get it? I found it one night in the fields around Abu Kabir. It was hungry, and I didn't know what to do with it. So I took the horse to Obadiah . . ."

The magistrate knew that Meylekh was not telling the truth but hiding some important fact. Meylekh continued: "Please listen, Your Honor! In my whole life I have never had anything to do with the courts. I have never been taken away like this with chains on my arms. I wanted a wife and was looking for a way to set up a home. She is a good soul, Obadiah's daughter. Judge me. Then I will know that I am being punished for what I did."

As he was being led away under guard, he caught sight of his wife, who was standing there enveloped up to her eyes in a black shawl, weeping silently.

Obadiah shouted out, "Liar! You've tricked me into giving you my daughter!"

"Meylekh, I will guard our house with my life, and I will look after the garden," said Zahara.

The magistrate heard her words and called back Meylekh and the policeman. "I will let you go free on the condition that within a year you pay Obadiah the full price of a horse."

That night they drank arrack in Hassan Salim's bar. All of Yussuf Tsalakh's friends were there. Even the Arab Mohammed al-Zahari came, and at the head of the table sat Swarthy Melekh with his wife. Yussuf drank the first glass with Obadiah's daughter.

"I am not angry with you anymore, Yussuf," she said. "I swear it on my life, as there is a God in heaven." Yussuf Tsalakh shed tears of happiness. He embraced Meylekh and danced around in a circle with him, singing Yemenite songs. Even the Arabs Mohammed al-Zahari and Hassan Salim and their sons joined in the circle, and they celebrated until late into the night, emptying many bottles of arrack and cold beer. Yussuf paid for everything because a burden had fallen from his shoulders.

"Oh, Meylekh, my brother, what did I tell you from the very beginning? Do you remember? Without a ruse you won't manage to get a wife!"

Swarthy Meylekh did not remember anything because he was drunk, but it was a good intoxication; he rejoiced over his turtledove of Sharon, who had truly become tame and stayed with him in his yard.

The Quiet Man of Prophets Street

The passenger ship *Jerusalem* left at midday. Mount Carmel could be seen for a while, its white houses with their silver-green gardens reflected in the olive-colored water. I stood on deck, leaning on the railing, my face turned toward the Carmel and my back to the open sea.

"Have we left yet?" someone asked me.

I mumbled something without turning my eyes away from the Carmel, which I was gazing at obstinately, intensely, as if it were the first time I had ever set eyes on it.

"Oh, of course, we're just leaving the harbor." The person's voice was familiar to me. I had heard it before. Though I was tired, as I crossed to the other side of the deck my steps were light. I breathed in the sea air and had a vague, nagging feeling of regret. The sudden, muffled wail of the ship's siren cut away the last cords tying the ship to the port, and the long reflection of the Carmel shuddered and returned to its former place.

"We're already on the open sea."

It was the same voice, but I hadn't heard steps accompanying me to this corner of the deck. How had he gotten here, when just a moment ago I had been standing beside him on the other side of the ship?

I searched for the person who had addressed me. At first I couldn't see him because a thick pall of vapor had floated down from the white funnel just after the siren had sounded. But a moment later I spotted a man leaning over the railing, peering at the foaming waves as if he wanted to see his own reflection.

In the evening I was sitting in the buffet, reading the wine labels and discussing the different vintages with the barman while keeping an eye on the women who were walking around. Suddenly, in the glasses on the countertop, I saw the reflection of someone approaching me.

"I have spoken to you three times, but you refuse to answer me." His smile was at once friendly and challenging.

"Won't you sit down?" I said reluctantly.

"It's not very comfortable here," he replied.

We went over to a table that was separated from the others. He sat down diffidently and placed his slender hands on his knees. I looked at his long, pale face, his gray hair, and wide, blank, expressionless eyes. I realized that I *had* seen him before, but where? Perhaps on the quay before we embarked?

How many times have I torn images from the present moment and brought them back to my distant boyhood, persuading myself that they weren't happening in the here and now but had taken place in that long-vanished past—that they were not present reality but a memory that I was re-creating in vivid colors?

The barman was obviously right when he said that from one little whiskey cocktail one could instantly get intoxicated, especially at sea. Was I drunk?

"Would you like something to drink?"

"No."

"Barman!" I shouted. "Pour two glasses."

The stranger looked at me sadly.

"I know you; I know who you are," he said. "I have often seen you walking down Prophets Street—I even know which house is yours."

Hastily I took the glass and grasped it tightly in my trembling fingers. The fresh, soothing bitterness of the liquor cooled my burning throat.

I closed my eyes and saw myself walking down Prophets Street in the shade of the fig trees. I knock on my own door. There is the familiar face of a woman becoming stranger each time she looks at me. My shoulders are hunched. This morning I had stood on these steps, a quiet, unnoticed resident of Prophets Street. "Will I see you again?" she asked. I did not answer. Then came the scream of the ship's siren, and through the steamy fog I discerned the thin, bent back of a woman on the quay.

"Drink!" I said.

He put the glass to his lips. Oh, how familiar were his gestures!

"I don't recognize you, and yet . . . for a moment . . . You live on my street too?"

"Yes."

"Perhaps I have met you in the cool of the night, walking along the avenue of fig trees?"

"Yes. I also like going for a walk at midnight. At that time you can feel a little breeze from the sea."

"You are a quiet man," I said in a mocking tone. "Even on the ship I couldn't hear your footsteps as you wandered around in the fog."

"A quiet man?"

His pale face flushed red.

"Forgive me, but you are wrong. I see you are slightly inebriated." He walked away, leaving his glass almost untouched.

I remained at the table listening to the distant jazz music and watching the dusk gathering. I invited a young woman to my table. "Please sit down. Do you speak Polish? Let's welcome the first evening in the Mediterranean together."

She had a pleasant smile, and I was surprised at my unaccustomed boldness.

Large brown eyes, curiosity, and warmth; chestnut-brown hair flowing down her long neck. She hums along to the tune on the gramophone, and now and then she addresses disjointed remarks to me. She comes from Kraków; during the war she hid on the Aryan side. Now she lives in Montreal; she has been on a visit to Israel. "I have experienced difficult times—you understand? Divorced . . . Would you like to see a photo of my cousin in Israel? Perhaps you know him? Do you like the looks of him? I'm going to Paris . . . meeting a friend

... he's a psychiatrist. He wants me, but I . . ." She starts humming the *cha-cha-cha* melody again, then adds quietly, "He's already been married twice . . ."

Irritated, I call out to the barman: "Pour me that cocktail you were recommending!"

I wander unsteadily up the stairs, holding on to the banister.

"When do we sail past Crete?" an elderly man asks me.

I stare at him without answering.

"I think it's tomorrow morning," he answers himself.

How lonely ship passengers feel! They have such an urge to talk; they search out other people in order to have some human contact in a universe of sky and water.

It's late at night.

In my cabin I can't sleep. The regular drone of the engine is accompanied by the monotonous sound of the sea.

Someone slowly opens my door, and I see a shadow creeping along the wall.

"Excuse me, but I can sense that you are not asleep. I am your neighbor. We already know each other. Would you like to have a smoke?"

"Thank you, but I don't smoke."

"Are you angry that I left the table without a word and without drinking the wine?"

"I really didn't notice your departure."

"Really . . . ? Really . . . ?" After a moment of silence he seemed to become uneasy and asked again: "You are not angry with me? That's good—I see you're not a petty sort of person. Oh, it's hot tonight; there's a khamsin blowing over the sea . . ."

I was overcome with exhaustion and felt totally indifferent to the sound of the night sea and the human shadow moving along the sloping cabin walls. Everything suddenly became distant and strange. "Who are these two people in the dark cabin?" I thought to myself. "One sitting silent and humble, and the other dozing on the bed. What's the name of that drink I had in the bar? I think it was a

Bloody Mary . . . I wonder if that Jewish girl from Kraków and Montreal who's traveling to Paris will smile at me again . . ."

I bit my lips and began to harangue myself. "How pathetic and empty you are—that's your true face." Why had I slammed the door of the house on Prophets Street and turned my back on her? Why did I wander around in the shadow of the fig trees and sycamores for nights on end, unraveling my wretched past like an old rug, trying in vain to weave new, brightly colored cloth from it?

"Yes indeed, there is a khamsin blowing on the sea," I said.

He was pleased that I had answered him. He came and sat on the edge of the bed.

"Earlier today you called me a quiet man and said that I wander around in the fog. I'm not going to tell you my name—it wouldn't mean anything to you in any case. I'm just a neighbor of yours, a companion on the voyage. So just call me 'quiet man,' call me 'neighbor,' that's a suitable designation for me. Today I told you that I know you, and in fact I do know you well. I know that you are a writer, and I have read your books. I haven't just read them; I've also often accompanied the hero of your work, and you too—I was like your shadow."

I heard the gramophone again, and I couldn't tell whether it was real or if the memory of the young woman in the bar had summoned it.

"Don't be surprised—every human being has a silent companion, hardly visible. He doesn't persecute him or speak to him. Sometimes the companion disappears—and when that happens the person is engulfed by loneliness and begins to feel lost. Now, between sky and sea, I have met you face to face. Here there are different laws than on land. We're on a floating island and none of us can escape. For both of us the world has become so small and narrow that for the first, and perhaps the last, time we have to break our silence."

"What do you want from me?" I asked.

"I want nothing from you, nothing at all. I just want to talk with you. If you had had this talk with yourself, I would have remained silent, but you won't. I'm certain of that. I know your works, and I see how you depict your life, how you narrate your days and nights. Only I can confront this. Only I—"

"No, you can't, because I myself can't distinguish between truth and illusion; everything is so bound together. And in any case, what's the point?"

"To take stock of yourself. But you are unwilling to do that. You haven't the courage or the strength to see yourself as you really are. Even though you constantly talk about yourself, you are still concealed. This night, on the ship *Jerusalem*, I want to help you to uncover your true face."

I sat up hastily and felt the warm breath of my neighbor.

"Leave me in peace; I want to go out on deck. Why are you pressuring me? And why tonight? I'm tired; I've probably drunk too much. Is it not possible to open that porthole? No, of course, the waves are splashing on the glass—we would be flooded."

But all my willpower seemed to have deserted me, and I leaned against the wall; my head had grown heavy, and it sank onto my chest.

The man jumped up; *that's his first victory,* I thought. I was filled with apathy. The words of my neighbor mingled with the waves and pounded against the dark porthole.

He spoke quietly: "I remember your last day in Warsaw during the German attack, the heavy air bombardment. We met in the same air-raid shelter in a cellar in Karmelicka Street. You were a soldier in the Polish army. You were captured one night by the Germans, with about twenty of your fellow soldiers. The lone Jew among the captured Polish soldiers somewhere near Okęcie . . . An old Polish woman weeps before a German officer: 'Please let me give this package to my son!' The German agrees. She stands in front of the captured Poles and doesn't know who to give the parcel to. Suddenly her eyes meet yours, and she cries out: 'That's my son!' You took the little bundle with indifference and laid it by your pillow. In the middle of the night, when you were all waiting for the trucks to take you somewhere far away, you undid the little bundle and saw that it contained civilian clothes. You put them on furtively, in the moments when the guards' searchlight shone above you like a knife. Then you lay down again and dozed. At dawn, when the prisoners were being loaded onto the trucks, a German soldier pulled you out of the line. 'A civilian! What are you doing here?' He prodded you with his rifle butt. You turned your back on your fellow prisoners and went away. Do you remember that? Do you remember the face of that old Christian woman dressed in black?"

"Yes . . . yes . . ." I stammered. "Yes . . ."

"And yet you never wanted to remember your escape that morning. Why? You don't speak? You don't want to answer?" He laughed. "Do you remember, you stood at the doorway of your home in Warsaw, and your mother said to you, 'Don't leave me here alone,' and your youngest brother begged you, 'Take me with you!'—but you banged the door and went off, following the war through towns that had just capitulated to the Germans, until you reached Russia . . ."

"Don't torture me," I begged.

"I'm not torturing you. You have to speak openly about all this. It's time you did."

"There was nothing else I could do . . . When I turned my back on my fellow prisoners, dressed in these strange civilian clothes the unknown old woman had given me, I was terrified. I thought that any moment the German guard would open fire on me . . . How could I have taken my mother and brother with me on my desperate flight across war-torn lands? I could only expose myself to the dangers, alone."

"Don't try to defend yourself. Your words accuse you, so why try to defend yourself at the same time? I know that your self-justification is only for appearance's sake. You've never been capable of defending either your own life or the lives of those close to you."

"That's a lie."

"A lie, you say? That's rather excessive. Think back to the moment when your neck was being squeezed by that terrible man in a dark corner of a station in the Moscow suburbs."

"Be silent," I whispered, recalling once more those bony fingers, the musky smell of his animal breath, the red-veined whites of his little swampy eyes.

"It was in the winter of 1943. You had jumped off the troop train, the tin pot clanking in your hand. You ran to fill it with boiling water. An old railwayman was checking the wheels. 'Where's the boiling water?' you asked him. He only gestured that you should get back into the carriage. But you ran on. Someone ran after you, shouting, 'Turn to the right!' You turned to the right, and then a second man materialized, saying, 'Behind that fence you'll find the hot water taps.' You were hungry and thirsty, you were wearing a greatcoat, and when you reached the wooden fence someone suddenly grabbed you by the shoulders and put his hands around your neck so that you couldn't breathe. Someone else pointed a knife at you. *This is the end,* you thought, and you didn't try to cry out or struggle. The pot fell on the snow, and your hands hung inertly. You couldn't scream; your limbs were paralyzed. Only your eyes were alert. They were wide open and gleamed like candles that flare up for the last time before guttering out. What feelings did they express? Submission, supplication, despair, apathy, anger, joy, thankfulness, and hope. The large drops of sweat on your face shone like rubies. Then suddenly, the unbelievable happened. The fingers that were knotted around your neck loosened, and once again you breathed in the frosty air and the scent of death. The man shoved you away from him. 'You're lucky,' he said in a hoarse voice. The other put his knife back in his pocket, and you bent down slowly, picked up the pot, and said to the two men—"

I threw myself at the quiet man who had been pursuing me on the ship.

"I don't want to hear what I said then. I don't want to . . . I want to forget all about it. Why are you rummaging around in my past? Get out of here and leave me alone!"

My hands fumbled around in the darkness, but I simply could not manage to touch the quiet man in my cabin. Had he already left? Perhaps I should turn on the light. Where's the light switch? I groped in the darkness but couldn't find it.

And again I heard his voice:

"You said to those two men, 'Thank you . . . thank you.'"

Tears welled up in my eyes and there was a tightness in my throat. "Yes, it's true. I said, 'Thank you.'"

He came nearer in a confidential manner, and his words kept time with the slapping of the waves against the porthole.

"When you got back into the carriage the old railwayman followed you. Polishing his cracked glasses, he crossed himself and said quietly: 'Give thanks to God, young man, that you were saved by a miracle. Do you realize you were in the hands of bandits? Every day in this quiet station they murder and rob a few of the soldiers from the passing troop trains. In exchange for a greatcoat or a pair of army boots they manage to get a loaf. The authorities turn a blind eye. God be praised.'

"You listened to the old man with indifference, extracting a piece of hard bread from your bag and chewing it. Your lips were whispering, 'Thank you.'"

"Go on, speak; I'm not going to struggle anymore. You've launched your attack against an exhausted man, one who is agitated by all he has experienced. You saw me drinking wine, and you're making use of the opportunity. You take pleasure in that, my worthy neighbor, Mr. Quiet Man."

"No, I take no pleasure in it. I am the person who is closest to you, and it causes me pain—that's why I am speaking to you. I know that you are suffering. I have often seen you bowing your head humbly before men wearing boots. You have even whispered their praises with trembling lips. And when you entered the free world again, you were unable to get rid of your fear and submissiveness—they became a part of your life. You start up when your name is called out; every knock on your door makes your stomach turn over. Every letter you receive makes you nervous, and you tear it open with clammy, trembling fingers. You long to be among people, but when you are in their company you sit locked in your silence. Though you like having friends, you mistrust them because you mistrust yourself as well. You simply can't find a place for yourself under our radiant sky, and you constantly expect something bad to happen. You are still afraid of that unknown, faceless person who will come one of these days and fasten his fingers around your neck again; in everyone's jacket pocket lurks the gleaming knife. At night you smell that frosty scent of death and you start up in terror, without remembering or understanding where this nightmare comes from.

"You still can't walk away from your doorstep, your mother's cry of 'Don't leave me alone!' and your brother's plea. Those worn-out clothes that an old woman gave you when you were in the hands of the Germans—you're still wearing them. You are still walking around with the same bent back and hunched shoulders as you did in Warsaw when it fell. Even now you have turned your back and are walking away. But I knew this would happen: you are always someone who walks away, never someone who arrives. Don't worry; I will never leave you. I will accompany you, for I know that you'll come back. You must come back . . ."

When I got up it was already broad daylight. I went out on deck. The sea was silvery-blue as far as the eye could see. I was alone; it must still have been early. A sailor went past, his face fresh, coppery-brown. I took deep breaths of the sea air.

"Have we left yet? Are we just leaving the harbor? Are we already on the open sea?"

Did someone ask me these questions yesterday? Was it a mirage? No, it wasn't a mirage; I was talking to myself.

Only the barman is real, he and his refreshing cocktails; the Bloody Mary is real, as is the young woman with chestnut-brown hair and the music that the loudspeakers will soon play all over the rolling ship.

"Come to my table!" I called to her again. "There are two full glasses waiting. You are going to Paris? There you'll meet your . . . what did you decide during the night?"

I laughed and realized with horror that those sounds were an echo of that laughter in the night that I'd heard from my "quiet man"—my neighbor.

"Do stay at my table," I said to her. "You'll save me from my boring neighbor who just won't leave me in peace. Look at the shining sea—it's like glistening amber."

The Ice Floe

I stood in the open doorway of the Russian cottage and said, "Akim Prostavilin sent me."

A peasant woman with broad Mongolian features and heavy jowls stared at me curiously.

Everything seemed very familiar to me: her dark-colored Russian peasant dress, decorated with gleaming white lace; the kitchen smells; the glow of the fire in the stove; the walls' brown pine beams; and the little lamp illuminating the smoke-darkened icons in the corner. The peasant woman shook her head as if she pitied me.

Instinctively I looked at my hands, at my worn coat and my boots, encrusted with snow and clayey earth.

"Akim Prostavilin . . . from the village soviet," I repeated. "I have brought my wife from Tin'geshi . . . she's due to give birth tonight . . . she's in the village hospital. . . . Can I stay the night here? Akim sent me . . ."

She pointed to a wooden bench and left the room. I looked after her. Her swaying walk, the way the hem of her dress was raised over her calves, her neatly woven bast shoes—all of this made her look younger. After a while she came back with a bundle of hay and spread it over the bench. I noticed that her brow was furrowed and twitching nervously.

Was it because darkness had suddenly fallen, or was it just that my eyes were so tired after a whole day of staring at nothing but snow and more snow, and my horse's back? Was this why I suddenly imagined the peasant woman was not spreading fragrant hay for my tired body to sink into but instead dark shadows?

"Yevdokha Stepanovna, thank you . . . I just need to rest my bones . . . my horse kept sinking up to its belly in the snow . . . ten whole versts . . . what a blizzard . . ."

I was waiting for Yevdokha to say something, even just a murmur of agreement as a sign of welcome, but she remained silent.

"Who knows how a journey like that is going to turn out?"

No answer. I heard her footsteps in the hallway and saw the fire in the stove dying. She went silently over to the icons in the corner and crossed herself, and then I heard her voice for the first time as she prayed with hoarse, broken words that gradually turned into whispers. Then, by the shadow falling on the little blue windowpanes, I saw that she had climbed up onto the stove.

Somewhere in the distance a sheep cries out. I think I hear the howl of a wolf. Inside me the blizzard still rages. My breath is icy, and I feel as if I am a lump of frozen snow waiting to thaw out. The prickly fibers of ice that had stung my eyes are now weaving themselves together into a frosty web. I throw myself into this spider web of snow with hunched shoulders, trying to tear through it, but I can't manage it. I close my eyes and draw my coat over my face.

I hear a groaning from under an ice floe. Who is drowning? Will I be able to crack open the iron-hard sheet of ice with my bare hands? I call for help. Am I dreaming, or am I awake and really hearing this groaning? I am helpless. I can't open my eyes. They ache from the whiteness of the snow. Oh, they are open after all. I try to lift my arms, but they sink into the snow. The horse's back is covered with a silvery frost.

Who is that talking in the cottage?

I hear two voices: a hoarse voice and a woman's voice talking together. I strain my ears. It is not a dream but a real conversation. Now I can move my arms, and my eyes are wide open.

Suddenly there's a knocking at the door. "Open up! Open up!"

In vain I try to sit up. Should I light a match? In the pitch dark I fumble around in my coat pocket but can't find any matches. Then I remember that my pockets are sewn together because they were torn and the wind was blowing through them.

"Open up or I'll break the door down!"

An eerie silence. There's a movement on the stove. Again the shadows on the little windowpanes. Then I hear Yevdokha's muffled whispers at my bedside: "Oh, God, they've come. Oh, my God . . ."

Her whispering only lasted for a moment because the knocking started up again. I could hear fists hammering on the door.

An icy wind whirled in as the door burst open. Angry, hissing voices and muffled screams mingled with the howling blizzard. The bluish light from the windows went out, and I sank into a deep pit.

"Good people, please, don't kill me. . . . Oh, my God. . . . He's raising his ax. . . . Oh, my God . . ." That was Yevdokha's voice, and I suddenly realized that the strangers had come to murder her.

How many were there? I hear boots echoing on the floor of the cottage. A table being overturned. Muffled voices like a blunt saw cutting into an oak tree.

"Sa-a-a-a-ve me!"

A muffled scream coming from far off. No, not from far off—it is the sound of someone being strangled.

I hear the wind blowing the door back and forth. In an instant it will be all over. At this instant the ax is being raised—it's about to descend. I can't breathe. My arms are paralyzed. I hear myself scream. No, it is the screech of the door. It is the howling of the snowstorm. It is the cry of the sheep being devoured by a wolf . . .

"Ah-h-h-h!"

I tear through the frosty web of thin ice and can feel my hands again. I'll flee into the darkness. I'll smash the frozen windowpanes with my fists and wake up everyone in the cottages.

No. No. It is all over in any case. It's late. Curl up. Keep silent. Bury your weary head in the fresh hay. Calm down. What has happened in the cottage is only part of the storm. You can't do anything about it anyway. Cover your weary body with your coat and pray.

Don't ask God for anything, but thank Him and praise Him for granting you these tiny moments of life, for not letting the ax fall on your head. You are insignificant. You are an ice floe floating on dark waters. Before your eyes ice floes are splintering against shelves of ice; they crash around wildly and shatter like crystal vases hurled onto marble steps. You are an ice floe. Simply an ice floe. Praise God for letting you float in safety. The furious waves are carrying you along, and you can hear the cracking of ice. You are powerless. You are a fragment. Draw in your shoulders, hold your breath, for you are nothing but an ice floe . . .

Something heavy fell on the floor and rolled over. There was the sound of muffled breathing. The hoarse voices faded into the distance.

It really was all over. Yevdokha Stepanovna had been murdered.

The door swung on its hinges, and its rusty screeching reminded me of my nearby village and my little cottage; I remembered the torn harness worn by my horse, belly-deep in the snow. What was I doing in this cottage? Why had I spent a whole day battling the blizzard?

Oh, my newborn baby! I start up, trembling. My God! It must have come into the world at the exact moment the ax descended on the peasant woman. Yevdokha's dying scream and the newborn baby's cry had fused together in the night of the wild snowstorm . . .

I sat up and put my feet on the cold, frosty floor. The wind cut like a knife. Again I heard the howling of the wolf. The sheep had been devoured.

If I try to flee the cottage I'll encounter two burning, wolfish eyes. There is no escape for me—I have to stay here. No, you mustn't stay! Flee! Run away! You will be accused of committing the murder. Run to the little village hospital and find out if it's a boy or a girl. Run before daybreak. Otherwise you'll be tied up and dragged by the peasants over snowy fields to a strange town, to the magistrate . . .

I strained my ears. Perhaps I would hear someone breathing? No. Total silence. I could just make out a dark bundle in the middle of the room. I groped around for my clothes. Perhaps I had some matches? There still seemed to be embers in the stove. I could see a faint flickering on the glass that protected the icons, but it was as weak as the light of a glowworm.

"Me? Me? How can you say that? How can you?" I'm addressing someone in a pleading voice: "Me? Oh, God, don't accuse me of that . . ." I find myself trying to prepare my defense—or perhaps I am really talking to a severe accuser. And perhaps I am indeed guilty? Guilty because I am nothing more than an ice floe.

The little windowpanes were turning blue. The first flush of violet on the frosty, feathery glass. I jumped up from the bench, stepped over the black shape on the floor, and in a moment I was standing in the middle of the village street. Behind me there were dark traces in the snow leading from the poor cottage. I was shocked to see that they were the only footprints there.

"The only footprints," I whispered to myself. "The footprints of the unknown men with the ax have been snowed over, and only mine show up clearly. Are those not traces of blood?"

Should I shout? No, perhaps I should run to see my newborn child. What am I to do? I must run. But I am no more than a piece of ice, a lump of snow carried along by the stream.

Run!

Who is giving me that order? My fear, perhaps, cracking a leather whip over my head.

From the chimneys, thin wisps of smoke are snaking into the sky. I race down the village street. My footprints will betray me, and I can't escape them. I am alone in the village's dark gray dawn.

A sickly yellow light shines from a window. I bang on one of the shutters. No one opens it. Here are some stairs to a porch. I rush up, tear the door open, and find myself in the middle of a brightly lit cottage. A kerosene lamp throws a circle of light onto the ceiling. Peasants are sitting around the table, and among them I recognize

Akim Prostavilin, the broad-shouldered head of the village. I stand in the middle of the room and feel as if I'm about to scream, but instead, strangled words come out: "Yevdokha . . . where you sent me to stay the night . . . Yevdokha Stepanovna, she was murdered after dark . . ."

Akim looked around at the other people at the table and said in a sleepy voice: "Don't be alarmed, stranger. . . . Look at your clothes. . . . You've got no hat, and you're covered with hay."

"But I heard terrible screaming. . . . Stepanovna was struggling. . . . I think there were two or three of them . . ."

The village head burst out laughing.

"Come and sit down at the table. Have a cup of tea from the samovar." My hands are shaking so much that I can't hold the cup.

"I am innocent!"

Akim calmly sipped his tea, and between mouthfuls he explained: "Yesterday I forgot to tell you that Yevdokha has these strange fits at night . . . it comes from her childhood. She endured a Tatar attack— her whole family was stabbed to death. From then on she constantly has these terrors: she relives every detail of that attack night after night. Please don't be angry: I completely forgot to warn you. She has had three husbands, and they all left her; they simply couldn't stand these attacks of madness every night. During the daytime she is completely normal."

I walked along the street and saw that the snow had covered my footprints leading up to Yevdokha's cottage. My horror disappeared with the darkness. But something of the ice floe still remained within me.

Kuzma the Muzhik

The storm started at harvest time. First came the rain: slanting, deluging, as if a waterfall were pouring from the sky. Then the hail battered down—icy hailstones and lumps of snow as big as pigeon eggs. At last, on the third night, the wind blew up.

"It will drive away the clouds. It's a good thing."

"What? A good thing? It'll flatten the fields."

"It will tear the grains out of the ears of wheat."

"Afterward we'll have to go around the fields with baskets and gather it up . . ."

"In any case the harvest will be late, for there are no muzhiks left in the village."

"Ach, the war . . . over there the young folk are being slaughtered, and you, God in heaven, are trying to wear us out with hunger here . . ."

"Don't blaspheme, Starukhe . . ."

A willow tree was torn out by the roots, and Mikishkin's gate had been broken down. Stopikhe's barn had shifted more than two feet and the roof had fallen in. For several hours the cow had been bellowing, and Stopikhe was forced to bring her into the cottage. The wind had torn off the roofs and scattered the straw from the stacks. The harvest was doomed.

"The whole summer long we haven't had real workers. The women can't make the haystacks properly. How can they understand farm work?"

They were standing around the extinguished icon lamps, staring at gray windowpanes that were illuminated every few moments by the silvery light of the torrents of rain.

At daybreak, the brigade leader of the kolkhoz knocked on all the doors. "Everyone come to the kolkhoz's main yard."

By this time the storm had abated, and all the damage had to be repaired. Who would do that? The old men, or the youths, the fifteen- and sixteen-year-olds?

During the night, the roof of Kuzma's house had caved in, and at dawn some of the old men came and lifted the paralyzed old man from his bed on the stove. The ceiling beams were broken, the walls had crumbled, and the chimney lay in the middle of the ruined cottage.

They carried him into the yard, put straw on the wet ground, and laid him down. "It won't rain today," someone said.

Kuzma stayed there on his own. Because his wife was not right in the head they did not make her work in the kolkhoz anymore. All day she went around muttering curses and rummaging about with the poker in the empty stove: "You damned bitch, where have the devils dragged you to?" After cursing and screaming she would sta- tion herself at the foot of Kuzma's bed, still holding the poker. This lunchtime she lit a fire and made a hot meal for her crippled husband. He ate the thick buckwheat porridge, drank some cold water from a ladle, and looked at his ruined dwelling.

He had been paralyzed for fifteen years. He could only move his arms. He was able to carve wooden spoons and weave slippers from lime bark, but he was unable to walk a single step. His legs had be- come shrunken, his head was large and smooth like a pumpkin, and his skin had darkened to the color of tobacco. Even his voice seemed to echo out from a cavern.

Sunny days came again, and everybody was busy at the harvest. Who had time to bother about the crippled Kuzma? What would hap- pen to him when the rains returned?

One evening the whole village rushed to see the miracle: the paralyzed Kuzma was moving all by himself. He was crawling on all fours. Then he stood up, holding on to the broken planks of his house. A fire flared up in his eyes. He is standing, God almighty! He's standing upright! His legs are twisted and shrunken like beggars' sticks, his body short and heavy. He's going to fall, and his huge bald head will crash against the wooden beam and shatter like glass!

But the miracle that nobody had foreseen actually happened: Kuzma spent the whole night sharpening his ax, which he had not held in his hands for the past fifteen years. He scraped off the rust and mended the nicks in it, and he also straightened the teeth in his saw. At dawn he started working. The ends of the pine beams were rotten, so he shortened them. The first few days he crawled on all fours, but after that he was able to stand upright on his sticklike legs. He kept stopping to rest, panting hard, and a thick, steamy breath came out of his nose and mouth.

It was going to be a tiny dwelling—about the size of a peasant's bath—but there would be enough room for a bed and a small stove. He had no choice, for where could he get new wooden beams? A little house like that would do for the rest of his days.

From time to time an old neighbor would come and offer to help Kuzma lift the beams and lay them on the semicircular cutouts he had made with his ax. The peasant women always crossed themselves when they passed his house. It was a miracle sent by God. Old Maria even swore that at midnight she had seen two white wings coming down from heaven. It was these wings that had brought his cure.

"What are you talking about, Maryukha? So many thousands of healthy muzhiks are dying in the trenches, and millions are lying wounded on the battlefields—all the angels are really busy, and at a time of war like this almighty God is not likely to bother about some old muzhik who has already been paralyzed for fifteen years and is on the way out anyway . . ."

"Ach, you poor creature, do you not even believe in God's miracles anymore?"

And yet the village did regard Kuzma's newfound ability to stand on his feet as a miracle of some kind.

By the time the potatoes had been harvested, Kuzma's house was ready. Again there was a ferocious storm like the one they had suffered at harvest time. First came the rain pouring from the sky like a waterfall. Then the hail battered down, the size of pigeon eggs.

Kuzma climbed up onto the stove, kissed the icon, and murmured his nightly prayer. And that very night, his first night in his little wooden house about the size of a bath, he died. The stove had warmed up, and as the fire in it expired, so too did the peasant Kuzma.

Reflections Beside a Young Pine Tree

The gallows was made from the trunks of two newly felled twenty-year-old pines. They were full of knots and jagged, broken-off ends of branches. The trunks were sunk deep into the earth. The soil too was fresh, a dark brown that was almost black—the real black earth of Ukraine. Across the two trunks was a pole, from which hung a noose.

The gallows stood not far from a mossy green fence, beyond which the misty blueness of a forest stretched away into the distance. Fresh green already showed in the fields, even though little islands of snow still lingered in the hollows.

Low, blue-washed Ukrainian cottages: shingle roofs, gray straw, rusty metal. The market full of puddles. Little wooden bridges over a slimy green ditch. Tiny windows collapsing toward the damp earth. Creaking doors. A path of scattered, uneven stones leading to the church.

Old men were gathering at the gallows. They leaned their backs against the fence. Along the broad road leading from the big village of Pustomiti came several trucks. A tank that made a sinister, disturbing noise drove not along the middle of the road but on the edges of the fields, smashing the bushes and part of the fence, knocking down a row of cherry trees, and dragging a bundle of barbed wire from someone's garden.

Its grinding, metallic noise was eerie because it made no echo; rather, its sounds were deadened by the damp, soft earth. The misty forests in the distance absorbed the tank's wailing with a defiant indifference that was devoid of fear, in contrast to towns, where all the windows rattle and the houses tremble, the pavement splits open, and the walls are broken down by its steel tracks.

From the trucks sprang armed soldiers, who ran to the gallows.

I am standing among the peasants. They look at me suspiciously. A stranger? In a military uniform? Who sent him here? Their silence swells up. Something will happen soon. They will fall on their knees, screaming and lamenting. I see them recoiling from me, first with their eyes, then physically, as they mass together. From their perspective I belong to the "Soviet authority," for I am indeed wearing a Russian uniform.

One truck has driven right up under the gallows. A young Ukrainian, about the same age as the pine tree from which he will soon be hanging, wears a light-colored sheep's fleece and stands in the center of the platform, surrounded by Russian soldiers. I watch them tie his hands and put the noose around his neck. I hear his short, stifled cry: "Long . . . live . . ."

One of the soldiers punches him in the face. A small trickle of blood runs down his cheek, which looks to me as if it has been split open.

Suddenly the truck accelerated and drove off, circling around the gallows. The hanged man swung to and fro, the trunks and cross pole of the gallows swaying with him.

The peasants crossed themselves. I wanted to look away from the gallows, but some strange force made me remain there until the end. The tank drew near, and an elderly Russian captain stepped out of the uppermost hatch and stood on the turret. His movements were calm and measured. He combed his fingers through his dark beard, his other hand in his bosom. There was an eerie quiet. Even the dangling man hardly moved. We were waiting for something to happen, and I had the feeling that the bearded officer on the tank was also waiting. And strangely, as soon as I heard a cock crowing on the other side of the mossy fence, this thought came into my head: *As soon as the cock stops crowing, he will begin to speak.* I was right, because as soon as the silence returned he took a roll of paper from his breast pocket, put his right foot in front of him, held up the paper, and unrolled it. His voice echoed, sharp and metallic. I half expected to hear trumpets blaring or the roll of drums.

The whole scene of the bearded captain on the tank opposite the gallows took me to a distant place. In a painting I had seen something similar. It reminded me of the great spectacles that took place in Roman amphitheaters. How everything repeats itself! How does it happen that a military judge imitates history like that? His every movement, his voice, and the unrolled paper scroll made me realize that the world has remained the same from time immemorial. Everything is natural: just as trees blossom, so do gallows. Everything is immortal. There will always be crucifiers and crucified.

I had been lost in thought for so long I hadn't noticed the villagers returning to their homes. I hadn't heard the trucks departing. I felt a hand on my shoulder. The elderly captain stood beside me: "I see that you are grieving for him . . . do you regret his death?" He laughed.

"Regret?" I repeated in surprise. "I know very well what these fanatical young Ukrainians have done. This people has been seized by madness. During the Nazi occupation they declared war on the Jews, the Poles, and the Russians, and when they saw that the Germans were losing they were ready to wage war on the Germans too. They murdered their own Ukrainian brothers. Who knows how many the bands of Bandera and Bulba killed? Hundreds of thousands . . . perhaps a million. . . . And yet I tell you, Captain, it is a vile world . . ."

I turned up my collar and prepared to leave. What nonsense! I was in danger of starting to philosophize and let my tongue run away with me . . . to hell with it! What does revenge mean anyway? To hang a village lad and destroy two lovely pine trees in the bargain? Is it possible to extract vengeance for all the things my eyes have witnessed? It's a drop in the ocean.

"Come on, let's have a drink."

I followed him silently. We sat at a bare wooden table and clinked our glasses, then ate some black bread.

"Captain, you gave a magnificent reading of the judgment of the high military court. You really seemed to be living it. It reminded me of the past—forgive me, but you are presumably a lawyer by profession, a judge perhaps, or did someone recommend you for this role? Please don't be angry at my asking you, but what is your profession in civil life?"

He took his time answering. He drained his glass of vodka and said: "I am an actor."

Laughter from the Skies

We drove over the Sydney suspension bridge, which had caught my attention from afar with its strange gracefulness. It looked as if it were suspended on chains of silver mist. Our car snaked along roads from which one looked down over calm ocean bays with white sails and green, hilly shores. As I stared into the distance, I suddenly realized that we were on the bridge that had fascinated me from the first moment I had arrived in Sydney.

Once again, broad streets with big shops. Lines of cars at intersections where the lights were red. At last we got out of the city and drove east. Our goal was to reach the desert, the dead heart of Australia. I was traveling with someone who knew the route very well, as he had crossed these wild places many times, going as far as the city of Darwin in his truck. That was about fifteen years ago, when he had come from the German camps and had a job driving truckloads of cement from the factories. Now he was the owner of about a dozen vehicles, with drivers working for him.

We had estimated that the expedition would take five days.

The landscape changes quickly. One minute we are driving through mountainous territory covered with small bushes and low, stunted tamarisks and the next we are among eucalyptus trees. The road is elevated and we can only see the treetops, but when I lean out of the car window there's a dark chasm with a forest of eucalyptus. A kangaroo stands unperturbed at the side of the road with its two short front legs raised. "She's trying to hitch a ride," laughs my companion. He's a man in his early forties, already a little gray at the temples and with a few silver strands in his jet-black hair. As I look at his hands grasping the steering wheel, I see that they are the experienced hands of a good driver and mechanic.

About midday we arrived at the plains. The wide, bare horizons stretched in every direction. There was nothing to see except the road, which had been tarred a while back. Brownish-green grass, gray, clayey earth. Dried-up bushes and the withered remains of flowering plants that were a product of a short-lived spring.

As the daylight began to fade we arrived at a sheep farm. An Australian with a wide-brimmed felt hat hanging from his shoulders greeted my driver with an embrace. I stared at the long raccoon tails on his hat, and at the wooden pens for holding the sheep, the pools of water, the broken-down cars, the heaps of wheels, tires, iron, and rusty tin. Nothing was growing here, not a single tree. As the wind drove the dust clouds along the ground, they shimmered with a coppery-gold color.

We washed at the taps and then ate our meal together with the shepherds at long tables. On a wire above an extinguished fire hung a sheep. I was given a fork and a long knife, and I cut off a piece of mutton. It smelled of eucalyptus, of smoke, of dried blood, and of the bitter desert dust. Then we drank wine, which cooled our blood, and went to look at a dried-up riverbed that would be full of rushing water during the rainy season. There were veins of gold there, said my companion, and when darkness began to fall you could see the gold dust shimmering out of the dry earth.

"Let's wait till it gets dark," he said.

In silence we watched the last remnant of light disappearing in the west. "Where are the sheep?" I asked.

"They're dozens of kilometers away, but they get driven back here at shearing time."

When night fell the plain was enveloped in that first darkness that is denser than the darkness at midnight, and I saw little grains of gold glittering on the dry riverbed. I was drawn to it and wanted to touch it with my fingers.

Behind me I heard my companion laughing. I was holding a handful of sand and letting it run through my fingers, for as soon as I grabbed them these grains of gold turned into sand. He was sitting near me on the ground and laughing with an echoing, hoarse laughter that seemed to ricochet against the distant darkness and come back to me. It echoed in my ears long after he had stopped laughing. I noticed that he also seemed to hear these echoes of his own laughter, and I sensed that they made him sad.

Around midnight I started up from sleep, woken by wild, mocking laughter that repeatedly receded into the distance and then approached again. It came from above, as if the sky itself were convulsed by mad laughter. I felt hot, and I could not rest comfortably on the hard shepherd's couch. I crept out of the eerie cabin and looked up at the sky. Through translucent silvery clouds birds were flying, and it was from them that this laughter was coming. They swooped down low above the roofs of the farmstead, then flew up again. I gazed at the desert. The earth was now gleaming with the light it had absorbed during the course of the day. The flatness of the open spaces fascinated me. It seemed as if the horizon were so close that you could touch it, much more so than during the day. I started walking alone, desperate to get away from the low clouds where those birds were flying around, laughing their insane laughter. I thought that a hundred meters farther on I wouldn't have these black night birds flying over my head, and I'd be able to await the sunrise with an easy mind.

When I got to the bushes I again saw the dry riverbed gleaming with the glittering dust; it was as if the Milky Way had fallen from the sky. Suddenly a shadow emerged from the darkness, and I heard a quiet voice: "I didn't want to wake you . . . I knew that you would get up and wander over here. Were you trying to escape these birds that fly over the farm after midnight? Did their laughter frighten you? As soon as they see a human being, they gather and circle around high overhead, then swoop down with their mocking laughter, which makes you shudder . . ."

Before he had finished speaking two birds descended, cutting through the dark blue with their shimmering blackness, and their familiar laughter rang out.

"Come on. Let's walk," I said.

We walked along this terrestrial Milky Way, which snaked along, often forming semicircles and sometimes a loop like a hangman's noose. We followed these meanders until we arrived at the open road that ran through the desert and looked at that moment like the blade of a steel knife.

My friend remained stubbornly silent. From time to time I made a remark just to be sociable, but my words produced no reaction in him. He unbuttoned his shirt and wiped drops of sweat from his brow.

"Come. Let's go back," I suggested.

He stopped and looked at me silently. Once again I heard the mocking laughter from the sky. I bent over and put my hands over my ears.

"I invited you to come and see the desert because I wanted to talk to you . . . This conversation must be here, in the desert itself . . . I must tell my story to someone. I've been preparing myself for a long time. You must hear me out. Don't ask me why it has to be here, in the desert. That will be clear to you later, when I've told you everything. When I saw you wandering away toward the desert, in exactly the direction of the place it happened, I knew without any doubt that I had to tell you now, during the first night of our journey."

He looked up angrily at the birds and pointed to the sky: "They were the witnesses to that meeting. I feel that since that night their laughter has become even more mocking, more insane . . ."

Though I did not speak, my silence was full of thoughts that flashed through my head like lightning: Was it a wife who had left him? Or a lover? A friend who had betrayed him? Some other kind of catastrophe? An ambush in this dead heart of Australia? Memories of the camps? Or perhaps he was the victim of hallucinations during these midnight hours?

"Stop!" he shouted.

I looked at him without speaking. I was searching his face for some element of nocturnal bewitchment or the reflection of bright horizons. But I saw nothing except wrinkles at the corners of his eyes and the normal tiredness of a human being at midnight.

"It happened here, at the farm, the year I arrived in Australia. I had been in the German camps. After the liberation a distant relative helped me to get an entry permit. In the UN relief camps I had trained as a car mechanic and driver. I drove trucks on this route and often passed by the sheep farm. It was a sleepless night like this. Two trucks laden with building materials were parked at the side of the road. I got out of my vehicle. In the yard they were already roasting a sheep. The old farmer had a second means of livelihood: he rented out beds for the night to drivers and prepared for them a supper of roasted mutton and wine. He gave me a knife and fork and I sat down by the fire. The two truck drivers, who were also staying the night, were already sitting there. I was really tired and didn't feel like getting involved in conversation, so I sat apart from them and watched how the fire illuminated their hands and faces. Suddenly I heard that they were speaking German to each other. My curiosity made me draw closer, and I went up to the fire and began to cut myself a piece of meat from the roasting sheep. I recognized one of them: it was Sepp Butke, the German guard in my camp. Sepp . . . that specter . . . I threw pieces of wood on the fire, and the flames leapt up. I hurled all the wood that was lying there onto the fire, and the faces of these two men stood out brightly against the shadows, so that I was able to see Sepp clearly. He was older, but it was definitely him. Suddenly, he started shouting in English, and then changed almost immediately to German: 'Hey you, *Donnerwetter!* You'll burn the sheep to charcoal! What are you making a blaze like that for?' His shouting revealed him to me completely; I had no doubt at all who he was. It was the same yelling that I had heard so often before; a face can change, but not a yelling voice. It was he!

"Soon after the liberation I had found out that Sepp came from Lower Bavaria, from a town called Falkenstein. I met a comrade from the camp, and together we traveled to Falkenstein, four hours by train from Munich. We found Sepp Butke's house. We wandered around the town for a whole week and learned that Sepp was alive. At night we dreamed of how we were going to take revenge. However, it turned out that he didn't live in that town anymore. But now I had discovered him. I knew his ugly mug very well. We had even collected photos of him: Sepp in the Hitler Youth, as a flag bearer, as a soldier of the Reich, Sepp with his fiancée, with his comrades. And now here he was, sitting by the fire holding a piece of mutton. He sprang up and started stamping out the fire with his boots, cursing. I kept silent, and only the birds' manic laughter could be heard.

"I wandered around the farm all night. I went out into the desert and walked until all the landmarks disappeared: the farm, the trucks, the low bushes. Then I started back, arriving just as the first gray light of dawn was appearing. At dawn both of the Germans came out of the bunkhouse. Sepp started up his truck and drove into the desert. The other German drove off in the direction of Sydney."

My friend sat down on the ground. I stood opposite him and waited patiently for him to continue speaking. I knew that this encounter could not possibly have had a happy ending. I started imagining how the story might conclude. Or perhaps there wasn't any real ending? Maybe that was why the experience weighed on him so heavily?

"Just there, where you are standing—that's where I squashed him with the wheels of my truck, there, on that very spot."

He stood up and quickly moved away from where he had indicated. "It happened right here! I pursued him with my truck, overtook him, turned my truck sideways on the road, and extinguished the engine. He was seething with rage. I yelled, 'Hey, you come from Falkenstein, in Lower Bavaria? Your name is Sepp? Answer me!'

"I didn't hear his answer because he started up his engine with a harsh noise of grinding metal.

"'Sepp! Out of the truck! Out!'

"I took my revolver out of my pocket and screamed, '*Raus vom Wagen! Raus!*[1] I'll shoot! *Raus!*' He got out of his truck and put his

---

[1] "Get out of the vehicle! Get out!" (In German in the original.)

hands up. *'Ich hab' nix . . . kein Geld!'*[2]

"'Hey, Sepp, I've been searching for you for years! Do you remember me from the camp? You bastard, you tortured hundreds of my comrades. Your moment of reckoning has come, Sepp . . .'

"I saw him shrinking, cowering, and like a cat he sprang back and started running. I pursued him in my truck. I steered with one hand, and with the other I aimed at him with my revolver. He ran along the road for about fifty meters. It took time for me to accelerate, and when I caught up with him he turned and ran, zig-zagging, into the desert. I drove after him, my truck bouncing and skidding, and several times I thought it would turn over. Sepp was running fast. He turned around from time to time, and I shot in the air to scare him. But I knew that his end had come. I would crush him with the heavy double wheels, after I had completely exhausted him. No, he wasn't going to have a quick death by a bullet. He was going to die as slowly and painfully as had my youngest brother, whom he had stoned to death in the quarry. I had found that out from witnesses. No, not with a bullet . . . I screamed: 'Hey, Sepp, your end has come! Run, Sepp! Faster! You're just about to die like a dog, and the mad birds will laugh their heads off!' My shouting echoed over the desert, mixed with Sepp's screaming and the noise of the engine.

"He was almost under my wheels but managed to get away once more; he tried to cling to the truck's door, but I beat his fingers with my revolver until they bled, and he had to let go. He collapsed beside the truck, near the front wheels. Again I shot. He writhed like a worm thrown up out of the earth into the light by a sharp plowshare. He clutched his head, then his body. When I accelerated in order to circle around and get him with the wheels, he stood up again, evidently realizing that he hadn't been hit by the bullet, that he wasn't bleeding and was still alive. He started running again. 'Ho-ho!' I yelled, and the desert echoed back: 'Ho-ho!' How long was this going to go on? I had one bullet left, and I wasn't going to waste it by shooting into the air. Sepp fell again, and my truck rushed past him at speed. Clumps

[2] "I have nothing . . . no money!" (In German in the original.)

of earth flew up, accompanied by clouds of dust and smoke. Suddenly Sepp realized that his own truck was not far away, on the road, and he began to run straight for it. I accelerated to about a hundred kilometers an hour and drove at him with all my force. The front wheels went over him. I felt the soft mass of his body as the truck bumped over it, and then the double rear wheels crushed him. I wrenched open the door, jumped out, and saw that Sepp was lying with his face buried in the desert sand. The blood was seeping out of one side of his crushed skull, mixed with brains and sand . . ."

"The desert birds were flying around just as they are now. They circled over Sepp, laughing maniacally. I haven't driven on that road for a long time. I had to tell this story to someone, and I feel better now that I've told it to you. I've been waiting for ages for an opportunity to talk about it, and now I feel as if I've freed myself from something. Do you understand, I probably wouldn't have taken revenge on him in that way if he hadn't yelled with that same voice when we were sitting around the fire. I would probably have reported him to the authorities—but they wouldn't have done anything to him; he would have gotten off with some kind of penalty. Why did he yell like that at the fire? . . . No, I don't know why. I . . . I'm not going to stay in Australia—I can't stand the laughter of those birds . . . they're mocking me . . . cruelly mocking the whole human race . . ."

When we drove back from the desert, that dead heart of Australia, it was late at night. The suspension bridge now looked to me as if it were hovering together with us over a chasm.

A Man in a Cloud of Dust

"Did anyone in your family survive?" I asked.

He put down his heavy tankard of beer, laid his hands on the table, and was silent. You could hear the Bavarians at the long wooden tables sucking on their pipes.

I had been in this little German town, Wörth, for two days. A friend of mine from the American occupying army had his headquarters here, and I had come to visit him. He was on duty at that moment, and I had time to wander around the little streets and country lanes. I encountered a young man.

"*Amkho?*" I asked.

He looked at me with an air of suspicion that turned to curiosity, until finally he seemed to trust me.

"You are American? Have you dollars? Would you like to exchange them?"

My light-green military-looking clothes had evidently given him the impression that I was a UN official.

"No," I answered, about to walk away. Then I looked more closely at the young man. He was certainly no more than twenty years old, dark-skinned with sharp features and curly black hair.

"I come from Volhynia," he said. "Are you not from our region?" And before I had time to reply he added: "I'm from Korets."

I approached him again and said, "I know Korets. I presume you were there?"

We went down some steps into the bar. It was dark, and pipe smoke floated around the massive ceiling beams. A German woman with a pretty face and short, bare arms put brown tankards on the tables and opened their lids.

"We lived on the market. My father was a wood merchant . . ."

"I knew him," I said softly. "I remember your sister. I was a teacher in the neighboring village of Ludvipol." Then I asked the question: "Did anyone in your family survive?"

After a silence he exclaimed: "Why are you tormenting me with this question? You know everything that happened, after all."

"Yes, I do know everything."

He jumped up.

"What do you know?"

I looked at him with a mixture of surprise and pity. Why had I embarked on this conversation? I wanted to repair the damage I had done with my question, but I didn't know how to go about it.

"You said you knew everything, and now you remain silent. You don't want to accuse me to my face, like others do. I'm sure you've been told about me. I know that you're friends with the American Jew who is the commander here. Was it he who told you, or someone else?"

I didn't know what he was talking about nor why he was so upset, and I had no idea what he was being accused of.

"When you spoke to me just now on the street it was in order to start up a conversation. I assumed you wanted to talk to me about the German woman I'm living with, who is now my wife. But now I see that you don't know anything about this. Not yet, anyway. You'll know about it sooner or later. Not only is she a German, she is the daughter of an SS man who is wanted by the Americans. Your friend has been in our house many times. They've searched our home. I knew this SS man, Willy Handke . . ."

I paid for the beer and left the bar without saying anything more to the young man. I had three hours to kill until my friend returned in his military jeep. I walked off toward the hills that rose up just behind the fence. Thorny bushes, sandy patches. Between them, a narrow, tarred path with red-roofed houses surrounded by greenery. The young man from Volhynia followed me on his motorcycle.

"Go away!" I shouted.

He skidded to a halt in the sand. His face was fiery red, but his lips were pale and trembling. "You have to hear me out. I want to tell you something I haven't ever told anyone. Someone has to know the truth. . . . Don't push me away; I am innocent . . ."

He sat down on the grass and started tearing up grasses by the roots and crushing them between his fingers. He began to speak: "Handke was the commander of our village. I was his message boy, his servant, because I spoke German. I used to carry the parcels that he often sent to his family: 'Elfriede Handke, Wörth, Lower Bavaria.' I frequently wrote the address on the parcels myself, and then I took them to the post office. I was on my own. My parents were murdered. When they were exterminating the Jews, I managed to hide. I would repeat the address quietly to myself: 'Elfriede Handke, Wörth . . .'

"Two of us survived, myself and a comrade, and after the liberation we were determined to take revenge on Handke. We crossed the Polish border, stayed in UN camps in Austria, and eventually arrived in Lower Bavaria. I found the Handkes' house in Wörth, but he was not there. I learned that he was still alive and wanted by the Americans. We took a room in a small hotel not far from his house. For days I stood at the window, noting when the shutters were opened and closed; I watched the daughter go shopping or leave with her mother to go to church on Sundays. I desperately wanted to get inside the house. Perhaps I would discover where he was hiding? I wanted to see what they had in there, for instance their clothes and jewelry—I remembered what the Jews had been forced to give him. Once he demanded a box full of gold, which my father brought to him. We had filled a box for keeping nails with people's wedding rings, watches, and earrings and given it to Willy Handke.

"My friend didn't want to stay there any longer. 'It's madness to keep on watching this house in Wörth,' he said, and left. I remained, alone. At first I was the only Jew in the little town, but gradually others arrived. The UN sent regular food parcels, and I also obtained food coupons. Your American friend got me all sorts of good things.

"I got friendly with my neighbors, the Handkes. I gave them real ground coffee and American cigarettes. They invited me to their house, and I went, bearing gifts. I had to find out where the murderer was. He was still alive, after all. I wanted to insinuate myself into his household and burn it down, but only after having defiled it. I wanted vengeance for my murdered parents. I had already planned how I would burn down the house. I had bought a motorcycle so I could have access to gasoline. I even worked out from which side I would enter, in through the porch, in order to set it alight. The best time would be three o'clock in the morning. That was precisely when our ghetto had gone up in flames, during the last murderous operation.

"But I kept putting it off day after day. I worried that his neighbor's wooden house would also be destroyed by the fire; in it lived an affable, elderly German with whom I had chatted on several occasions. He was a comrade of Liebknecht's, and a son of his had died in a German concentration camp. I became a frequent visitor to Handke's house, and one day his wife suggested that I should stay in one of their rooms. I accepted."

The young man from Volhynia fell silent. It seemed like he was searching for words, that he wanted to continue speaking but didn't know how to express himself.

"I started sleeping with her. She came to my room that first night. She was a forty-something German woman but as submissive as a servant girl. The more insolent and arrogant I became with her the more humble she became toward me, just like a degraded slave. 'Ha ha! Willy Handke, look at me—I've stamped into your holy of holies with my boots! I'm going to screw your daughter too . . . that's the best revenge on you, Willy Handke, you, member of a superior race. . . . Look at your wife groveling at my feet! Ha ha!'"

His laughter sounded like a howl of anguish.

"And so six months went by. The daughter became pregnant by me, and I began to see her face changing. The—to me—disturbing, alien features of the so-called superior Aryan race, as they believed themselves to be, started becoming familiar, and I saw her as just a suffering human being. I heard her soft weeping and felt her fear of the impending birth. Even her mother had changed: 'I was too old for you,' she said. 'It was a sin.' Both of them went to church every day.

"I couldn't bear the girl's quiet sobbing. I reassured her: 'I will marry you. The child will not be a bastard. I want everyone to know that it's my child.'

"In fact I also had an ulterior motive. I wanted everyone to know that Handke's daughter had a child by a Jew. I would marry her before a priest and all the inhabitants of Wörth! The wedding took place in the church. I stood there like a statue, my lips pressed together, secretly mocking the whole spectacle. 'As soon as the child is born, I'll be off, I'll leave Wörth. Let them bring up a Jewish child!' I said to myself. But however weird and incomprehensible it may seem, I was unable to carry out this plan either . . ."

"Where is Willy Handke?" I asked after a long silence.

A farmer came past, driving a few cows. In the distance the rumbling of trucks could be heard.

"I don't know."

"You do know!"

He lifted up his motorcycle.

"Ha ha! None of you will ever find out where Willy Handke is. He has already got what was coming to him . . ."

The motorcycle revved up, and his words sounded out above the noise of the engine: "Willy Handke is kaput . . . Willy Handke has received his punishment . . ."

The young man disappeared in a cloud of dust.

The Fiery Cross

"Checkmate!" called out the young Kazakh, Abakidze, gripping the yellowed ivory rook in his fingers.

"Let me take back my last moves. Don't be in such a hurry," urged Nikolai Kazantsev, the staff officer, who was not happy to be beaten so swiftly in a game of chess by this Kazakh, this peasant from a kolkhoz . . .

"Don't rush me, Kazakh . . . there, I've fixed it . . ."

The shooting outside died down. The Germans had been retreating since the early evening, but they were covering their retreat with artillery fire that was now receding farther and farther into the distance.

"That means they've already reached the far side of the Elbe," thought Kazantsev. "Well, they've managed to save their skins, anyway."

In the German village the soldiers were already celebrating. The military administration had discovered a warehouse full of wine and distributed two bottles of red wine to each soldier.

It was the middle of April, and a mild, early spring breeze was stirring the squeaky metal cockerel on top of a building. Russian soldiers sat outside on the stones by the big wooden cross where the crucified Jesus hung. They drank from the bottles and stared at the church. Its dark brick walls cast a shadow. The wooden cross with the carved Christ was draped with withered garlands and thorny twigs woven into crowns. From the barns the sound of drunken singing, and the long, drawn-out melody from a harmonica, drifted out.

Suddenly the door burst open and a soldier from the medical corps entered the room. She wore no greatcoat nor belt, her hair was disheveled, and her face was scratched and bloodied. With muddy hands she buttoned up her torn jacket and stood trembling before staff officer Kazantsev.

"What has happened?" he asked quietly. The girl could not restrain her sobs.

"Come on, speak! What is the matter with you?"

The soldier raised her tousled head. She was young and rather plain, with a prominent forehead, a flat nose, and a wide mouth full of large teeth. She looked at the two men, then at the military maps, the pictures, the papers lying on the desk. She seemed unable to open her lips and get the words out. A typical peasant girl from the Volga area. Abakidze recognized her; she had dressed a wound of his during the winter months in Poland.

"I've been raped," she said quietly.

Kazantsev stood up and took his revolver out of his pocket.

The room fell silent. Now the singing of the drunken soldiers could clearly be heard. They would be celebrating until the small hours after having driven the Germans back to the other side of the Elbe. The echo of the guns had faded away, replaced by a familiar air from the Urals, from Nizhny, played by Kolya on his harmonica.

"Who did it?"

"It was our soldiers—from your division. They dragged me into a barn . . . they were drunk. . . . No, actually, they weren't all drunk. . . . They tricked me . . ."

Kazantsev started forward. His face turned fiery red with rage. "Get out of here! Get lost! Get out, you whore!"

He banged on the table with his revolver and shouted: "I don't want to see you again! Get lost! It's not nurses we have here but prostitutes! You wanted them to 'rape' you—you led them on, and now you come to me . . . get out!"

The young woman put her hands over her face and retreated from the room. By the time she left, the dark-blue dusk had fallen.

The young Kazakh wanted to go back to the vehicle workshops and find a quiet corner to finish the letter he was writing to his mother. Before the war he had been training to be a teacher, and he hoped to teach afterward in his village. Today, the staff officer Kazantsev had summoned him to prepare the German Ford for a long journey. In the officer's house he had noticed a carved ivory chess set in a glass-fronted cabinet. He had learned to play chess from a beggar who had once been to the holy city of Mecca and who used to be the mullah of the neighboring village. When the prayer house was closed, the old man took to wandering around the villages and spreading the word of Allah. When the officer saw the Kazakh lingering by the cabinet and staring at the chess set, he asked him, "Can you play chess?" And so the game had begun.

"Don't rush away, Kazakh. . . . Let's finish the game. . . . I'm taking back my previous moves. . . . There, that's where my pieces were before," the officer said in a calm voice.

Abakidze was astonished to see how quickly the officer's voice and facial expression had changed: an air of calm benevolence now pervaded his features, and he smiled at the young Kazakh, treating him as an equal.

"Checkmate!" exclaimed Abakidze. "The game's over!"

He left the house and started wandering around the village. Where was the female soldier? He felt he had to find her. It seemed that during the pauses in the drunken singing emanating from the barns and former German houses, where Russian soldiers—*our* soldiers—were rowdily celebrating, he heard the quiet weeping of the unhappy, plain little Russian peasant girl. He went into his own small room near the village's workshop and glanced at his unfinished letter: "We are winning. Don't worry, Mother. The war is nearly over. Good times are coming." He tore it up and went out into the street. Where was she? What was her name?

The wooden cross loomed over the big German village. The crucified one looked down at his own bleeding feet, which were pierced by an iron nail. The street was empty, apart from the soldiers on guard duty, who walked up and down the street, back and forward.

The weeping of the young woman had taken hold of him, and he could not free himself from it. Why had Nikolai Kazantsev burst into such a rage? For what reason? *I see it all now,* he thought. *"Good times are coming?" What a lie!*

When he went back to the garage, he suddenly noticed a can of gasoline. He grabbed it and returned to the center of the village, where the big wooden cross with the crucified Jesus stood. The Kazakh hid in the shadow of an iron fence, and when the guard had passed he ran up to the cross, poured gasoline over it, and lit his little cigarette lighter.

Flames shot up.

The street was illuminated by a hellish light. The wood, which had been drying for centuries, flared up with a hissing and crackling.

"Will he fall, the crucified one, or will he be burned on the cross?"

"Let's have a bet on it!"

"*Ladno,* I bet you three bottles of genuine German schnapps that he'll be burned upright, just as he is, hanging on the cross!"

"No! He'll fall!"

The cross did not fall. The flames blazed more intensely, tearing the night sky, and then slowly began to die down.

"Jesus Christ has gone back to heaven!" shouted someone.

In the nearby barn the harmonica was playing ancient Russian melodies, and the Ukrainians were dancing Cossack dances. Abakidze wandered along by the shadowy walls, talking to himself. *We don't need gods anymore. The time is coming when they will be totally superfluous. They've been destroyed in our village and everywhere the revolution has reached. Why should these people here still have a god? The time is not ripe for Him yet, so He might as well go back to heaven in flames ...*

The Kazakh stopped at the open door of a barn, where sappers and tank crews were enjoying themselves. *The battle's over. We've won—we've chased away the Germans. They turned the world into chaos—well, who cares? Let chaos reign!*

"Hey," he said, "let me have a go—make room for me. I'll dance a real Kazakh dance for you! Come on, Kolya—play your harmonica!"

Abakidze started bawling out his guttural melodies, spinning around wildly while drunk soldiers stamped time with their boots and clapped their hands. The Ukrainian harmonica player and the Kazakh dancer were having the time of their lives.

Cain Laments at Night

Winter 1944. The Eastern Front extends along on the far side of the river Horyn. At night the sound of artillery fire can be clearly heard. On the snowy fields, footprints lead into the woods and distant hamlets. They are the footprints of the Banderovtsy, Ukrainian nationalists who range lawlessly around the villages and little shtetls that have just been freed from the Nazis. They attack Russian trucks, break into isolated military posts, and murder the last remaining Jews.

Emmanuel, a twenty-year-old Jewish lad, was staying in the little shtetl of Tuchyn for the night. There were four of them in the truck. The officer, Khromov, had received an order not to travel after sundown. They were to leave the shtetl at dawn and drive to Rivne.

In the evening Emmanuel wandered around the burned-out market. The wooden houses had been destroyed by the fire, and all that remained were little snow-covered heaps of mud and the walls of a prayer house. On the broad main street, gentile houses stood intact. On the sandy earth there was the fortified military base, a brick building that had once belonged to a Jewish doctor and was now surrounded by sandbags and coils of barbed wire. A Red Army guard stood there.

The young Jew couldn't rest. He was agitated by all he had seen and heard. Around midday his truck had been passing Korets, and Khromov had stopped the vehicle in the marketplace. Nearby stood Ukrainian women holding tin trays of pastries.

"Hey, Emmanuel, hop down and buy some of those pastries."

When he jumped down from the truck he looked around and saw the smashed-up doors and knocked-out windows of the Jewish houses—the crushed village—and in the middle of this devastation were peasant women with stalls made from doors and shutters, on which lay the black metal trays of Ukrainian pastries.

"How many?" the peasant woman asked.

"Ten."

The old woman bent down, took off her woolen gloves, and opened the cover of a large book. She licked her thumb and tore out a page. It was a yellowed page from a Talmud. Enraged, Emmanuel started, grabbed the page, kissed it with his frozen lips, and went back to the truck with the pastries. The four soldiers and the officer watched him in silence as he folded the piece of paper in four and slipped it into his breast pocket.

All the way back the soldiers made fun of Emmanuel, and Khromov drove the truck with such violent speed that a couple of times it looked as if they would hurtle into a tree or plunge into a muddy ditch.

In the evening, pork, black bread, eggs, and bottles of vodka appeared. The food was laid out on the table, and the soldiers poured themselves drinks and roasted the pork. A man blind in one eye sang a melody, tapping the time with his feet. Around midnight they sent someone to find a young Cossack accordionist.

Khromov had been avoiding Emmanuel. The whole evening the officer hadn't said a word; however, after he had drunk several glasses he started insisting that Emmanuel should drink, too. He peered at him intently and twisted his mustache with a cunning smile.

"Show me what it was you kissed . . . read it to us. . . . Are you a Russian soldier? No, you're a rabbi! Get over here, men! The rabbi's going to read us what's written in the holy pages . . . ha ha ha!"

Khromov was drunk. He staggered about. He laid a heavy hand on Emmanuel's shoulder and demanded the crumpled paper in his breast pocket.

The smell of the liquor, the tobacco, and Khromov's breath made the boy feel sick. He tried to extricate himself from the officer's grasp but failed. And then, suddenly, he felt a strong urge to read what was written on the Talmud page. But not here.

"I'll read it quietly when I am on my own, not with drunk soldiers, not at a table laden with *treyf* food," he thought to himself.

Emmanuel was not an observant Jew, but he did not want to defile the holy scripture—no! no!

"You bastard . . . you bloody—" The officer wanted to say something more, but he seemed all at once to have sobered up.

The accordionist started playing, and one soldier began to dance. He tapped out the time with the heels of his boots, squatted down until he was almost sitting on the floor, then suddenly, like a spinning top, twirled from one corner of the room to the other, slapping his hands against his boots and calling out with sharp, staccato cries.

The winter night looked in threateningly through the window. A desolate shtetl. Shadowy forests. Sandbags. Barbed wire. The guards' footsteps could be heard in the rare moments when the table fell silent.

Emmanuel wanted to leave, but he just couldn't because all around it was dark and here he could remain until daybreak. "Drink, little rabbi," Khromov and another officer insisted. "Drink. What are you thinking about, with your sad eyes?"

"This Jew is depressing. Come on, let's be cheerful; let's have another drink!" Suddenly there was silence.

The officers were signaling to each other and whispering. One of them left, and a few moments later he came back, accompanied by a small, deformed man wearing a short sheep's-fleece jacket with a turned-up rabbit-fur collar.

Emmanuel's brow broke out in sweat. He realized that this was one of the Banderovtsy killers who had already carried out massacres of Jews.

Khromov approached the small man in the fleece and prodded him with his revolver. "You son of a bitch! How many Jews have you shot?"

The Ukrainian cowered back, drawing his head into his collar. "I haven't shot any Jews . . ."

The echoing blow he received made the oil lamps flicker.

"I'm not guilty . . . the Germans . . . they dragged me with them . . . they forced me . . . as God is my witness . . ."

"You believe in God? Come on, tell us!"

"I believe . . . your honor . . . comrade . . . I do believe . . ."

"Ha ha! You believe in God, and our rabbi here believes in God, and yet you're slaughtering each other . . . ha ha!"

Emmanuel realized that Khromov was not drunk, even though he had emptied a whole bottle of vodka. The way he questioned the prisoner made Emmanuel sure that Khromov was a trained NKVD man.

"How many Jews were at the trench?"

"I don't know . . ."

The Ukrainian stood wide-legged, his head hanging, and his hands, which were bound behind him, trembled. His lips were pressed together and his beard stuck out as if electrified. Again Khromov prodded him expertly with his revolver. The accordionist played a couple of merry chords. "Maybe a thousand . . . men, women, and children."

"Hey, Emmanuel, come here! Do you hear? He took part in a massacre of your brothers and sisters. A thousand . . . children . . . women . . . men. . . . Why are you standing there with your arms folded? Do you want *me* to beat him up? What about you? Are you protecting your hands? Do you want to keep them pure? You can't drink. You kiss some ancient piece of paper. In war your sort aren't much use either. Surely at least you'll be able to take revenge? Ha ha ha!"

All the men burst out laughing, and the accordionist again started playing a tune that stopped and burst out again like crazy laughter.

"What are you standing there for? Shoot him!" Khromov shouted. "Look, he doesn't even want to take revenge!"

The Cossack twirled around and tapped the soles of his boots on the floor to the rhythm of the music, calling out repeatedly, this time with a mocking tone.

Emmanuel took his gun, slung it over his shoulder, and kicked the door open. "Come!" he ordered the Ukrainian.

The Ukrainian advanced, trembling. The door banged shut. The guards stepped back and let the young, armed soldier and his prisoner pass. It was a bright, frosty night, and the dark wood was menacing. From the brick building the sound of drunken singing rang out. They walked along the middle of the village street until they reached the fields. Emmanuel walked three paces behind the prisoner, his arm outstretched, ready to fire. He knew this was the way to the trenches and was amazed at the quietness of the night. You couldn't hear the artillery fire on the other side of the Horyn, and the prisoner was now walking faster.

They arrived at the edge of a half-filled trench. The Ukrainian stopped by the trunk of a young birch tree whose exposed roots hung over it.

"Here it is . . . this is the place . . . don't shoot me . . . let me live . . ."

He sank down to his knees, put his face to the ground, and started wailing.

Emmanuel stood over him. He felt the steel of the gun burning into his hands. He put his finger on the trigger.

The Ukrainian lay at his feet, moaning.

"Spare my life. I'm innocent. I was forced. I was deluded. I'm not the guilty one . . ."

Emmanuel took off his leather belt and bound the legs of the prisoner. At first he resisted with his elbows, since his hands were tied, but then he lay still. The whites of his eyes were glistening.

There was a piece of wire at Emmanuel's feet. He wound it around the knees and feet of the Ukrainian and then tied it to the trunk of the birch tree.

Dawn was already breaking when he returned to the brick building. The soldiers were slumped around the table and asleep on the floor. Khromov sat on a chair, wrapped in a rug. The lamp was flickering as the oil ran out.

In the early morning a truck rumbled up. Someone wakened Emmanuel.

"Get up. We're leaving . . ."

As the truck left, a peasant woman appeared from the path through the fields. She was crossing herself and crying out to Khromov: "There's a moaning and wailing coming from the trenches . . . it's been going on all night. Those are the trenches where they killed the Jews. . . . Oh! Good people! We are terrified. . . . The trenches are wailing."

Khromov fixed Emmanuel with a searching gaze and asked him sternly, "Hey, little rabbi, are the Jewish corpses lamenting?"

"It's Cain lamenting. Cain laments at night."

The Cherry Orchard

Soon after Passover, my uncle set off to rent the cherry orchard at Kołozab. He lifted me onto the two-wheeled carriage and put the reins into my hands.

"You're ten years old, so it's time you learned how to drive a horse and carriage." My uncle sat down comfortably behind me, took a little book of psalms out of his breast pocket, and started humming a melody. The horse picked its way carefully, because the road was sandy and uneven for a couple of miles. The winter corn was already high and green, and the wheat fields were dotted with cornflowers. The branches of silvery willows swayed along the roadside. To me they seemed to be moving to the rhythm of the psalms my uncle hummed.

From time to time I glanced at my uncle and was happy to see his contented face: he had a curly black beard and bushy eyebrows that met in the middle, and his cheeks were browned by the sun. He had unbuttoned his jacket, and his shirt was gleaming white, with the black fringes of his *arbe-kanfes* showing. When the willow branches stopped swaying in the gentle spring breeze, my uncle also stopped humming, looked around in surprise, gazed at the dark clouds on the far horizon, and said: "So, Master of the Universe, how long are you going to make me wait? Please send me a lovely little breeze—without it I can't remember the melody of the psalms."

The cherry orchard was in bloom. Even at a distance of two versts from Kołozab the breeze brought the fragrance of the cherry trees to us, and my uncle came to life. He inhaled deeply, his nostrils dilating and his eyes shining. He could not sit still in the carriage. As we approached, the stone wall of the landowner's house came into view, and just beside it the blossoming cherry orchard gleamed before our eyes, stretching right down into the valley where the river flowed.

It was about midday. A peasant led us between the rows of trees. It was hot, and my uncle took off his jacket. Every few steps he stopped and looked up at the trees, humming a little tune. I knew that he was calculating how many poods of fruit each tree would yield.

"Come here!" he called to me. "By the time I was ten years old your grandfather had already taught me how to estimate how much fruit each tree would produce when it is still in blossom. And you're already ten years old!" My uncle spoke so seriously that I suddenly felt I was grown up enough to learn all the secrets of a real fruit farmer.

"Look at the tree!"

I raised my eyes and peered up at it.

"What do you see?"

"A tree."

"Come on now, Mendel, don't play the fool. It's time for you to be a real man and understand these things. Do you see how the blossom covers the whole tree? It's not pure white but pinkish. That's a good sign. The bark is dark brown, with a reddish tinge in some places. That means that the tree is healthy and the fruit will not drop. Assuming that one branch will yield a whole pood of cherries, how much do you think, roughly, the whole tree will produce?"

I started calculating, bending one finger after the other, using my finger joints, even the little bumps and hollows, and eventually evaluated the harvest at twenty poods.

My uncle pinched my cheek so hard that it hurt.

"Oh my goodness, you're already a real fruit farmer! Your mother will be proud of you! This tree should indeed produce about twenty poods. But we'll have to estimate a bit less than that. Do you know why? Because we have to allow for possible storms or hail. Or the blossom could be attacked by a pest. You can't tell what will happen. That's why it's wise to calculate that the tree will produce about a third of that amount. And since the orchard contains two thousand trees like this, let's sit down together and make a thorough calculation."

My uncle started singing, and sang all through his calculations. He closed his eyes, rubbed his brow, and inhaled deeply once more as if he already smelled the fragrance of the full baskets of cherries. Then he got up.

"Come with me to see the landowner. I've made my calculation and I know how much to offer him for the rent of the orchard."

We sat on a wide veranda drinking tea. A dog was lying at my feet. The landowner talked with my uncle for a long time, and though I picked up a few fragments of the conversation, I couldn't really understand what they were talking about. The corpulent, red-haired Polish nobleman was asking why the Jews had been driven from their land. He twisted his mustache and screwed up his cunning little eyes.

"What's written in the kabbalah? Recite a few lines for me!" He smiled with an apparently interested expression and stared fixedly at my uncle's ritual fringes.

"Why has that holy garment you're wearing got black stripes?"

My uncle answered all his questions, drumming agitatedly on the table with his fingers.

"The black stripes? They are in memory of the destruction of Jerusalem."

The nobleman went on asking questions: "Is it true, Eliasz, that in your book of the prophets the coming of Jesus Christ is already predicted?"

My uncle's face went white, then red. He looked at me, and I realized that he was weighing his words carefully. He spoke in measured tones, quietly but firmly: "There is nothing like that in the Book of Books. The Jewish Torah is very open. Everything written there is crystal clear. What people draw from it is another matter. There is no other people so tolerant of other faiths than the Jews. Do you know, your honor, what the prophet Micah said? He said these words: "For all people will walk every one in the name of his god, and we will walk in the name of the Lord our God for ever and ever."

The Polish nobleman jumped up.

"Oho, is that really what's written? Show me it then, Eliasz."

They went into the house, striding quickly through the entrance hall decorated with stags' heads bearing antlers, and stood at a large cupboard full of books. My uncle took out the Bible in Polish translation, leafed through it confidently until he came to the page, and pointed at it with a reproachful finger: "There it is. Read it!"

The nobleman read it out loud.

"*Pravda!* It's absolutely true!"

It was very quiet in the room, and in the stillness I heard the voice of the Pole: "Eliasz, you're a cunning devil! You knew exactly what was written in my book."

"It is not your book. It is *our* book. . . . Your people just translated it."

The servant brought a bottle of strong wine. Even I was allowed a little glass of it. I was bewildered by the aristocrat's arrogance and his attitude of irony mixed with genuine respect toward my uncle.

When they began playing chess, I went out into the courtyard. I knew that my uncle would have to lose the game. It was the same every year after Passover, when my uncle came to rent the cherry orchard: the affair would begin with a religious dispute and end with a game of chess. The landowner had no one in the village with whom he could play, and if he lost the game it would upset him and my uncle would return without the cherry orchard. I didn't want to see the aristocrat's triumphant exultation when he won. A feeling of rage had come over me, and I couldn't shake it off. I plodded through the orchard all the way to the little birch wood and lay down on the grass. In front of me was the river Działdówka, to my right the blossoming cherry orchard, and all around me—long grass. Everything smelled of bog plants, mint, and the fragrance of the cherry blossoms. I tried in vain to visualize the devastated city of Jerusalem. I thought I heard the music of harps being played by King David and the daughters of Judah. I lay looking up at the sky, following the drifting clouds, and I felt as if I were sailing away to distant lands. The scents of spring invaded my senses and I began to doze.

I don't know how long I lay there sleeping on the damp meadow.

I was woken up by the barking of the landowner's dog and the voice of my uncle Elye calling me. It was already dark. I lay curled up in the carriage, covered by a rug, listening to the clip-clopping of the horse's hooves. My anger against the landowner had not gone away. I remembered his sarcastic words and his contemptuous smile and the way my uncle's face paled when the nobleman mentioned the name of Jesus.

I wanted to tease my uncle about his cowardice, so I said, "Hey, Uncle, I suppose you lost the game? Just like every other year . . ."

He did not answer, because it was time for the evening prayer, and his quiet whispering seemed to me even sadder than usual.

That night my body was on fire. The fever made me talk incessantly and writhe around on the bed. I imagined that I was fighting with the landowner, screaming, "Checkmate! Checkmate! You've lost! You're a fool! You don't even know what is written in your books!"

The barber-surgeon was called. Another Pole with a mustache like Kaiser Wilhelm in a portrait I had found in the attic.

"Stick out your tongue!"

I did as asked and then turned my back on the barber-surgeon. On the third day all my joints ached. I had a fever, but it was like a release because my hatred of the Polish nobleman burned more fiercely than the fever itself. In my nightmare-filled nights I saw flames engulfing his house. I saw him running across the fields in tattered clothing. I saw lightning strike his barns, which burned down. And in the middle of that storm I entered the nobleman's house and saw the stags' antlers flickering into flame. My body burned with heat and my lungs filled with smoke. Swift as a deer I ran to the library and seized the Bible—the same volume my Uncle Elye had leafed through to find the words of the prophet Micah.

They took me to a famous doctor in Warsaw. I remember the old Jewish Dr. Layfuner very well. He examined me, touching my inflamed joints and swollen knees; he peered at me very intently and asked me about my village, the cherry orchard, and the damp meadow where I had slept half a day during the springtime.

"The blood of this lad is mixed with the juice of the grasses, the sap of the tree roots, and the scent of the cherry trees," pronounced the old doctor.

Three years later, at my bar mitzvah, around Passover time, my uncle was going to Kolozomb in the carriage as he did every year, to rent the cherry orchard from the Polish landowner.

"I want to come with you!"

"All right, I'll take you, but you're not to lie down and go to sleep in the damp grass!"

My mother accompanied us. I sat silently in the corner of the carriage, not listening to my Uncle Elye's humming.

The same argument with the landowner started again. Again my uncle quoted the words of the prophet Micah from the Bible in the landowner's library. The discussion was exactly the same as three years ago. But when it was time for the game of chess, and the figures were being set out on the marble chess table, I approached the nobleman and said: "I also play chess. Perhaps your honor would like to play with me?"

My mother smiled at me affectionately while my uncle sat me down in the armchair. I played with daring moves. The smoldering anger inside me burst into flame. Before long I was shouting out triumphantly: "Checkmate! Checkmate! Checkmate!"

My uncle wrung his hands and murmured to my mother: "This year we won't get the cherry orchard."

We drove home silently. That year the cherry orchard was not rented out to my uncle. I was to blame. The landowner never let my uncle over his threshold again. "Your checkmate cost me too dear," grumbled my uncle angrily, every time we met.

A Ruined Fair

The annual fair was being held at Purim time, at the end of the month of Adar Sheni. On the afternoon of the day before the fair, old peasant women arrived with little sacks. They perched like gray birds on the square and opened their bags, which were full of all sorts of seeds, laying them in a row. There was black poppy seed, red beetroot seed (which looked like little dried-up pimples), carrot seed like silvery-gray ants, seed for early radishes, onion seed, pumpkin seed, and sunflower seeds. They had all kinds of bulbs from which lovely flowers would blossom. The peasant women sat there quietly and patiently, one beside the other, wearing colored headscarves, contemplating the distant fields that were already shimmering with the phosphorescent pale green of springtime. The evening sky held the promise of a fine day for the next day's fair.

The shoemakers and tailors were also preparing for the fair. Their stands were already packed up and ready to be taken to the market in the early hours of the morning: hundreds of pairs of boots made of Russian leather, men's shoes made of leather from Buka, and high, brown, laced boots for young peasant women. There were also boxes full of clothes: suits of coarse cotton cloth and riding breeches that could be laced at the knees. The cloth merchants had prepared their wares, and the shops all around the square marketplace had laid their haberdashery out on display. People would say their prayers as soon as it began to get light the next morning, and then they would immediately loosen the bars and rods from the shutters and doors and throw their shops wide open to the customers who would soon be arriving.

However, not all was calm in the neighborhood. The peasants in the villages had been stirred up against the Jews. No Jewish peddler dared to show his face around Koźmin any more. In Przyborowice, drunken goyim had overturned some stalls belonging to Jewish tailors. In the new town, young Christians had handed out leaflets exhorting people not to buy from the "Yids." In Glinice, a Jewish cattle dealer had been beaten up. Strange characters from Płock were roaming around the villages. They were rumored to be Christian students, including Germans from Poznan. They were spreading like an epidemic and inciting the rabble; those who followed them were the well-known louts and hooligans, the gamblers who would hang about idly in the fields every Sunday, playing cards and swilling down vodka like water. For years they had kept a low profile; they were scared of the fists of Hershl Khish and Mosharn the pigeon catcher, and of the glare of Yosl Keyzer the porter and his five brothers, sons of a widow who lived on Zielony Square. When these young men walked out into the market, flung off their jackets, rolled up their sleeves, and spat twice into their palms, the gentile riff-raff made off—not just from the market but right out of the town.

But now things were different. The police were protecting these hooligans, and it was clear that the power lay in the hands of those inciting hatred against the Jews. The peasants were afraid to go into a Jewish shop if gangs of troublemakers were loitering in the marketplace.

On the eve of the annual fair, between the afternoon and evening prayers, when long rows of peasant women already dozed on the paved square beside their little sacks of seeds, a small, poorly clothed peasant appeared from Synagogue Street. He was deformed and had a yellow, straggly beard with whiskers that looked as if they had been made from cheap, roughly cut tobacco. He stood in the middle of the market, looking around, then began to stammer. The droshky drivers were just getting ready for their evening fares because at about seven o'clock the train from Sierpc to Warsaw would arrive. They removed the nosebags full of oats from under their horses' muzzles, adjusted the seats, and checked once again that the wheel hubs were tight and the rubber tires had not slipped.

"Hey, what devil dragged you into town at night, Wojtek?" called out the droshky driver Itsik Yalekh.

"Oy, is that actually Wojtek? It looks more like some kind of strange monster!"

"They've sent him to spy on us!"

"Please! A pathetic creature like that?"

"Oh, I think he's going to do something—I can feel it in my bones!" exclaimed Zalman Drongal with irony.

The droshky drivers surrounded the little peasant and stretched out their hands to him. *"Dobry wieczór,* Wojtek!"[1]

"I am not Voytek . . ."

"Who are you, then?"

"How should I know?"

Zalmen Drongal squeezed his hand so hard that the peasant let out a squeal of pain. Then they left him in peace because he really was a pathetic, crippled little peasant who seemed to have appeared in the town for the first time. The whips cracked, the horses' hooves struck the cobbles so hard that sparks flew, and one after another the droshkies drove off to Płocker Street.

The little peasant began to walk slowly around the market. He came to Anshel's tavern and gawped with amazement at the sign with the big painted bottle of vodka. He stood there for a while scratching his beard with both hands, then took off his cap and sat down on the wooden steps of the tavern.

"Hey, what do you want, peasant?" Anshel, who was standing in the open doorway, gave him a push with his knee.

"I want a glass of vodka!"

"Get up! Come in, I'll pour you one, and then you can move on."

"I haven't any money to pay for the vodka."

---

[1] "Good evening, Voytek!" (In Polish in the original.)

The innkeeper laughed so hard that his suspenders slipped off his shoulders. He leaned against the glass door, slapped the legs of his boots, then pushed the little peasant: "Go on! Off you go, Voytek!"

"I've already said, my name is not Voytek. I'm called Longin . . . I'm from Kolozomb."

The innkeeper suddenly stopped laughing. He had heard a lot about the Polish landowner Longin, who had lost everything because of a woman. He had gambled away his fortune somewhere in France at the roulette tables and had come back an alcoholic. So this was he . . .

"Listen, Anshel. I won't leave unless you give me a large glass of vodka. I'll sit here on the steps of your tavern until I die. As God is my witness, I will sit here until I die . . . I'm telling you the honest truth . . . I swear to God . . . I'll die if you don't give me a drink of vodka . . . here, on your doorstep." The peasant gave a crafty wink and added: "I know the law. That'll make trouble for you . . . it would be better if you gave me something to drink—then I'll go away . . ."

Anshel the innkeeper bore a grudge against the village of Kołozab. One of his grandfathers had once been badly injured on the squire's land. That squire must have been this old man's father. Savage dogs had attacked the cattle dealer while the squire and his entourage sat on the veranda. And now that same squire's son was lying on his doorstep. Let him lie there! Had they not already sucked plenty of blood from the Jews? And their bloodlust hadn't abated. For how long had the Swabians been persecuting and mocking the Poles? And for how long had the Russian bastards not even permitted Polish schools and had wanted to Russify the whole country? And the Jews had helped the Poles, supported them in their revolts! They'd helped the rebels by distributing Polish leaflets! The Pozners, Jewish landowners, had enabled Pilsudski himself to hide in the village of Kukhari. And now these Poles were collaborating with the Germans, damn them! Who knew what would happen at the fair the next day if that damned pest was still lying on his doorstep . . .

"Hey you, get off my steps!"

Anshel did not dare to push him away with force. After all, he had once been the squire of Kołozab. *Let him just lie there,* he thought to himself. *He'll croak before he gets any vodka from me. If I give him one glass I'll never get rid of him.*

The innkeeper closed the shutters of the tavern, locked the doors, and fixed the metal bars in front of them.

Old Longin spoke quietly. "All right, I'm telling you that if you won't give me any vodka, I'll die. Our Lady of Częstochowa will hear my prayer and close my eyes . . . I will die here on your doorstep . . . and then you—"

Anshel spat and walked off. He did not want to have any further conversation with the goy. Every day he had similar exchanges with Polish peasants. But today, on the eve of the annual fair, he felt that this was different. . . . Perhaps, after all, he should have . . . if he had just let him drink his fill and leave! If he hadn't said who he was and mentioned the village of Kołozab, Anshel would have given him a glass of vodka and sent him packing. Indeed, he would have felt a good deal of satisfaction in seeing one of these arrogant Polish nobility, who were so full of a sense of their dignity, being brought so low . . .

The night before the annual fair the electric lights were burning in many of the houses. The tailors were finishing off their cotton trousers; the shoemakers were polishing their calfskin shoes and Russian leather boots. They wanted them to shine, because the peasants loved gleaming boots. The first minyan had started early; the tradesmen said their prayers speedily and began taking their stands out into the marketplace.

When Anshel the innkeeper came out through the kitchen door to open up his tavern, the little peasant was still lying curled up on the steps, his head nestled in the rabbit-fur collar of his hooded cape.

"Hey you, get up! I'll give you a glass if you'll just move on!"

He nudged the sleeping man gently and saw that the body did not move at all, not even a tremor. The innkeeper backed away hastily and looked at the little peasant. What was he to do? He really was dead. And even though he had felt quite self-confident, now fear swept over him.

Balcer the policeman was walking along Płocker Street. Anshel ran toward him, greeting him with a friendly *"Dzień dobry!"*[2] and a confident little smile: "Some drunk or other . . . been here since last night—he's lying on my steps. How am I to get rid of him? My respects, sir . . . it's going to be a great day . . . do come in and have a little drink with me . . . I think we're both too sober, don't you agree?"

A little crowd had gathered around the dead man: the street sweepers, a few caretakers, and the girl from the basement, who had been escorting a guest of hers to his carriage. They were all gentiles—a bad sign, thought Anshel. "They are already gathering."

"Heh heh heh!" laughed Balcer the policeman with a sly wink. "He thinks, does that Anshel, that he'll get off with a bottle of vodka." Then he shouted out: "This isn't a simple matter! This Polish citizen has been killed—murdered—and it's your work. You have a hand in this business, Anshel."

The market gradually filled with peasants. A stone shattered one of Anshel's windows. The troublemakers—the cattle drivers, the students, and the Germans from the agricultural colony—all gathered around. They upended the stalls of some of the tailors and trampled their wares. The shoemakers left the market. The cloth merchants snatched away their cases without unpacking them. At the corner of Kozia Street the five brothers stood with their jackets slung over their shoulders so as not to waste any time getting them off. In their pockets they had brass knuckles. Mosharn stood with his hands on his hips. A few cobblers' apprentices, with pitch-stained, leather-hard hands, were at the ready: let the rabble just dare to come to the corner.

The county doctor, together with an examining magistrate, sealed up the tavern. There would be a lawsuit. The little peasant was stretched out on the steps, and on his face was an ironic smile. All around him the mob was rampaging.

---

[2] "Good day!" (In Polish in the original.)

Yitskhok the Red

I don't know why I suddenly had the notion to walk along Dzika Street and Niska Street with my girl. Perhaps it was because I was familiar with Niska Street, as my uncle owned a house there—a stone-built, square building with four stories, where artisans, carters, and porters lived. I knew almost all of them because my uncle used to take me on his visits there. I remember the dark staircase, the long corridors with half-open doors from which the smell of soapy water and fried onions drifted out. Often I heard the hoarse, sharp voices of women shouting, mingled with the crying of children and the yowling of cats.

My uncle often brought me along when he went to demand the quarterly rent from his tenants. During these visits I would see large carts drawing up to carry away the night soil from the courtyard; then my uncle would quickly retreat from the courtyard, whispering to me: "I don't want the goyim to see me."

"Why not?" I asked fearfully. "Why not?"

My uncle smiled and confessed: "I made a mistake and booked three goyish drivers, when one would have been sufficient." I stood there holding my breath, listening to the drivers quarrel with each other. Very soon they would come to blows. The horses were neighing, the peasants shouting. The street was full of people. Beside us stood a woman carrying a bucket of water.

"Landlord, my tap isn't working. When are you going to fix it?"

My uncle knew every tenant and was well informed about their work situation and their family matters. He owned a first floor apartment on Dzika Street that he made available to his tenants for marriage ceremonies. Almost every Saturday evening, after the Sabbath had ended, there was a wedding there. A band from Wolińska Street played with such enthusiasm that they could be heard inside the walls of the Dzika Street prison. In his rented house, widows did not remain widows for long, nor divorced women divorced. Uncle's drawing room was at their disposal. "Get married! Celebrate it at my house, and you'll be enabling me to perform a mitzvah, a good deed!" Thus my uncle reasoned, while poor Aunt Beyle could only sigh and remain silent. However, she complained that the servant girl couldn't finish her housework. When my uncle heard this, he started shouting at his wife: "Don't sin, Beyle!" Then he burst into such a fit of coughing that my aunt threw up her hands and wailed: "*Oy, vey iz mir!*[1] Did I say anything? Did I blame you? For goodness' sake, I'm not even allowed to say anything to you anymore!" And my uncle's coughing fit ceased.

I hadn't seen my uncle for a good many years, and now, walking with my girl, I remembered those years of my boyhood when I used to come visit Warsaw from my village and stay in the alcove off the drawing room. I was present with my uncle at quite a few weddings. To this day I have not forgotten the clowns and wedding jesters; I can still hear their rhyming songs sung at the moment when the wedding gifts were presented. I can see before my eyes the carters from Niska Street and Smocza Street, the porters and paupers who got married in their landlord's drawing room. They came dressed in black, unbuttoned jackets and satin waistcoats. From one waistcoat pocket to the other drooped a silver chain hung with coins. As they spoke, the silver rubles jangled. The majority were short, broad-shouldered, bald men for whom 95-proof vodka was just a watery drink to which they liked adding a little bit of pepper. When the ceremony of veiling the bride took place, there was enough weeping and wailing to melt a

---

[1] "Oh, woe is me!" (a common Yiddish expression of distress).

stone. The women started it, but no matter how tough the men were, in the end they were all sobbing. At this point they became bosom friends and fell into each other's arms.

It was there that I first heard genuine Yiddish spoken and saw how ordinary people celebrated their festivities.

As I left Niska Street with my girl and turned down one of the narrow side streets, our way was blocked by several boys who shone pocket flashlights in our faces: "Come here for a minute—you're needed," one of them said with a strong Warsaw Yiddish accent.

They took us to a bar at the corner, and I realized they were young hooligans. I was scared, not so much for myself as for my girl. She lived in the fashionable suburbs. Her father was an assimilated Jew and her mother came from a Sephardic family from southern France. And here I was showing off, taking her around my famous little backstreets, now sitting with these lads in the bar. It wouldn't have been too bad if I had been there on my own, but with her?

A gramophone with a rusty horn was playing with a grating sound. We saw an individual with a red face, his shirt unbuttoned, his suspenders showing, as well as empty vodka bottles on the counter and a floor covered with trampled mud. A man in his late twenties, covered with freckles, with red hair sticking up in a tuft at the front, came right up to me and laid his hand on my shoulder.

"Do you know who I am?"

"No," I answered.

"I am Yitskhok the Red. . . . You come from Sochocin, don't you? Have you never heard of Itskele the thief? I recognized you from my shtetl, but you don't recognize anyone, eh?"

"Now I recognize you—you dazzled me by shining the light in my face . . ."

I realized this was the face of the miller's eldest son. I remembered that he had been taken away to Plonsk in chains and that I later saw him again somewhere after he had been released. I knew the miller very well. I used to lie in the meadow not far from their water mill, catching little fish. I heard that their red-haired son Yitskhok had become a thief and would stay that way till the end of his life. I often heard people telling the story of how Yitskhok the Red tried to rob the house of the Polish landowner of Gutarzewo, and how horsemen pursued him through the fields. When one horseman caught him, Yitskhok punched him between the eyes, leapt onto the horse, and led them on a chase that lasted all night. I was then only eight years old, but I can still hear the frenzied clatter of hooves as they raced through the streets. I peered through the hole cut out of the shutters in the shape of a crescent moon, and I saw the gentile horsemen pursuing the young Jewish boy—the miller's oldest son.

"Now I can see that you know who you're dealing with—you know who I am."

Yitskhok the Red moved away from me, looked at the girl, and sat down comfortably on the table. One of his subordinates locked the door of the pub and pulled down the blinds.

"Search him!" ordered Yitskhok. When one of the lads approached the terrified girl and tried to take her handbag, he sprang up, thumped the table with his fist, and shouted, "Take your paws off the young lady. She is not to be touched."

The one who had searched me laid my wallet on the table. In my breast pocket I had a little notebook full of my poems.

"That's all?"

"That's all," I answered, feeling guilty that this was all I had.

Yitskhok the Red looked in my wallet, took out the princely sum of fifty groschen, and burst out laughing.

"You take a girl out with fifty groschen in your pocket? Listen—your name is Mendel, isn't it?—don't be scared. Having you searched was just a joke. What I really wanted to know was . . . Mundek!" he shouted to the landlord. "Bring some vodka—the best you have!—and something to eat." He turned to my girl, speaking in Polish, "Panienka, do you want to hear a waltz or a krakowiak? Put on the gramophone." And when the bottles of vodka and beer and the snacks arrived, he started shouting again:

"Is this how you treat my personal guests? You should spread out the tablecloth! Bring out the silver candelabra that we got last night.

Don't be scared, the door is locked. The table is to be set with all the finest things. He is from my shtetl, and I'm showing him hospitality. I want the people of Sochocin to know that Yitskhok the Red is alive and kicking! God damn them to hell! I have a score to settle with them, for it's they who made me out to be a thief. Did I go to Gutarzewo at night to rob the landowner? It's a lie. I went because I planned to run away with his young wife. She was madly in love with me. She said to me, 'Izaaku, I will take your faith, I'll convert. You are my beloved.'"

The table was set.

"Light the candles in the candelabra!" said Yitskhok. "I want to see them burning."

The landlord opened a packet of tallow candles and fixed them into the candelabra. They burned brightly.

"Some good French wine for the young lady!"

As we drank one glass after another, the girl kept looking desperately at her watch. It was two o'clock in the morning. I tried to get up a couple of times, but Yitskhok commanded me to sit down again. "We're not leaving till the bottles are empty. Turn off the gramophone. I've heard that you write poetry—in fact I once saw your name in a newspaper. Read us a few poems out of your notebook."

"Stop making fun of me, Yitskhok. How can I read poems here? Leave me in peace . . ."

His face turned scarlet with rage.

"What do you mean? Do you think we aren't the sort of people you can read poems to? Why shouldn't we hear one of your poems? Who do you write for then? For idiots? Be quiet and listen, lads!"

I was pretty drunk.

"It's really late . . ."

I read one poem after the other, short lyrical poems about the awakening love of a nineteen-year-old boy.

Yitskhok the Red grew sad and said quietly to me: "I did not go to Gutarzewo to steal. I went there out of love for her . . . but she betrayed me. She testified to the court that I intended to rob the landowner. I didn't want to tell the truth—that she had persuaded me to come to her in the middle of the night. I was sentenced to five years. The first people to believe that I was a thief were the Jews of Sochocin, and I'll not forgive them for that . . ."

His voice was tearful. His face had become hard and full of furrows, like a field in autumn.

"Open the door! Call a droshky!"

A droshky stopped at the door of the bar. The boys helped us to get in. Yitskhok the Red bowed like a gentleman and kissed my girl's hand.

"Driver! Take the young lady home first, then the young gentleman. I'm paying—don't take any money from them!"

As the droshky rolled along Niska Street, I glanced at my uncle's house. Then we emerged into the broad avenues.

A Tragedy in Four Acts
and an Epilogue

I went into a dark cellar on the marketplace with my two older friends, neighbors who lived in the same building. It was a Shabbat afternoon in winter, and in the darkness of the cellar you could smell cholent and apples. The bakery was illuminated by a smoke-blackened electric lamp, and the little chambers where the farmer kept his winter fruit were double-locked and secured with metal bars. In this cellar, which belonged to a widowed dressmaker, the members of the dramatic society were assembled. I was there for the first time.

A column of light shone in through a little window high up on the wall. At a table covered with a flowery tablecloth sat the director, Fishl Yagode, a small, nervous young man who had been a soldier. It was rumored that he had played important roles in big-city theaters somewhere or other. I never would have imagined that this young fellow, a peddler trudging from village to village in peasant boots, already with a wife and two children, could appear before me on a Shabbat evening in a completely different role. I watched him leaf through a tattered little book, putting the pages in numerical order.

"We'll start now!" he announced in a loud voice.

It wasn't until I had gotten used to the darkness in the cellar that I was able to clearly see the faces of the people who were sitting on the sleeping benches, on the widow's bed, on the stools and chairs. There were lads from Kozia Street, Synagogue Street, and the New Market. There were tailors' apprentices, fruit farmers' sons, shoemakers, and young men who helped their parents in their little shops and market stalls.

"We are going to perform a tragedy in four acts and an epilogue." Fishl Yagode's solemn voice resounded in the cellar with a mysterious quality that captivated me from the first moment.

I was not quite sixteen years old, but because I was tall they accepted me as an adult who could join Yagode's theatrical circle.

"Here is the text of a monologue. Everyone will read it out in turn, and I shall assign a role to each person according to how he reads it." Then he added in a very Germanized Yiddish that sounded elegant to my ears: "I shall now proceed to the distribution of the actors' roles."

I began to see this poor country peddler and retired soldier in his high boots and brown jacket in a very different light. I sensed that he had a great deal of hidden theatrical knowledge and that the daily life of toil I witnessed when I saw him trudging along our street was not reality for him but a play, where he was only inhabiting a role. This was the real Fishl Yagode, sitting at the table in the cellar where his true personality was revealed to us. Even his voice had changed; one moment he spoke with a crisp Lithuanian accent and the next in elegant Germanized Yiddish. He used words that were unknown to me and enunciated them slowly but clearly. Then he would look around triumphantly, as if aware that he was revealing an extraordinary aspect of himself that none of us had known about.

The first person to read was my neighbor Zorekh, the tailor's apprentice. It was thanks to him that I was present there in the cellar. Only a wooden partition covered in plaster separated his workshop from my room, so I often heard him sing. I would listen to his songs about the wicked tsarist government, about young Jewish conscripts in the Russian army, about love and treachery, as well as songs about the bitter poverty of the "suffering proletariat." When I heard for the hundred-thousandth time "With hammer and iron proudly we stand / And break down the walls with our own strong hands" followed immediately by the refrain "We break down, we break down the walls with our hands," I sometimes felt like throwing myself against the wooden partition separating us to put an end to his singing! Let his fighting words flood out elsewhere and wake up "cold, indifferent humanity"!

"Now, Zorekh, read!" said the director in a polite but authoritative voice.

Zorekh stood up, went over to the circle of light that came in from the little window high up on the wall, and began to read: "You have trampled on my heart! You have robbed me of sleep! Oh, unworthy one, like a thief in the night you have stolen into my soul! You have laid waste my dreams like a storm that ruins blossoming gardens! My life no longer has meaning, for you are in love with another. Oh, revenge! Revenge! Thus screams my blood! We both must leave this world—now, this very moment!"

As he finished the monologue, Zorekh was supposed to stretch out his hand, which held a revolver, and Fishl Yagode would strike the wooden table three times with the palm of his hand.

I noticed that the widow, who had been sitting the whole time in the kitchen, took up a corner of her apron and wiped her eyes with it.

"You can play the part of the girl's father," decided the director. "You know why, Zorekh? Because you read with the intonation of the Sabbath prayers. Next!" he ordered.

Khaskl read the same text. Then he wiped his glasses, which had steamed up with his hot breath.

"You will play the role of the chief of police!"

The director looked around and saw that the widow was still wiping her eyes, and he said to her gently, in his elegant Germanized style: "Leytsho, my dear, be so kind as to take a pencil and note the roles that I am distributing." He smiled lovingly at her. I did not learn until later that Fishl and the widow were engaged in a secret love affair that had started when Fishl was a cavalryman.

After Khaskl it was Artsho, the son of a porter, who read in a harsh, hoarse, imperious tone.

"You will play the part of the new lover."

And now it was my turn to read. Already I knew nearly the entire text by heart, so that I didn't even need to look at the paper.

"Oh, he's good at reading . . . you'll be the prompter! Look, folks, we've managed to grab a real prompter! He reads correctly . . . has a good memory . . . doesn't stumble over the words . . . Leytsho, put him down as the prompter."

Next Arontshik, the barber's apprentice, stood up to read. I knew him very well because he worked in the nearby barber's shop, and he had sometimes shaved my hair down to the scalp as the school regulations demanded.

He was small, slim, and agile; a lock of his light, curly hair fell over his right eyebrow. He had protuberant eyes and nervous hands. Now he stood under the little window and read the text. At first his voice was angry, then it shook as if he were holding back spasms of sobbing. All at once he shouted out with the angry pride of a deceived lover, and finally his voice subsided into hopeless resignation, almost into a kind of serenity, like the dying away of a storm. Instead of slapping the table three times as usual to indicate the shots from the lover's revolver, Fishl just gave one hefty smack on the table and exclaimed: "This is the kind of person I need! He was born to play that part! Leytsho, write down his name . . ."

It was not necessary to discuss who would play the role of the beloved. Everyone knew it would be the cloth merchant's daughter, Marishka. She had already broken several hearts and changed her admirers a few times. She had a pale, round, cold face, and in her voice there was something that was attractive and rather frightening at the same time.

"Marishka is perfect for the part; you couldn't imagine anyone better."

The parts distributed, rehearsals began. I got the script from Fishl, and in one evening I devoured the entire text of the tragedy in four acts and an epilogue, which was called *Love and Passion*. Years later I found out that the drama was an adaptation of a French book. The adapter had replaced all the French character and place names with Yiddish variants, so that there was no Mademoiselle Francine in the Bois de Boulogne but instead the daughter of a Jewish religious teacher from a little shtetl called Wyszogród, where she met her lover.

Some of the more "sophisticated" members of Fishl's drama group rebelled against this play, protesting that instead of *Love and Passion* it would be better to stage Andreyev's *The Seven Who Were Hanged* or even Ettinger's *Serkele*.

Fishl had a good answer to these objections, however. He showed us a colorful poster advertising the play's staging at the Scala Theater in Warsaw, where it had been very profitable. And Marishka was a talented artist—she had in fact played the same part in the Scala Theater production. Apart from that, he assured us that this was not inferior garbage but a genuine "true to life" drama; such things did actually happen. And as soon as we had made a profit, we would turn to the classical repertoire, but we had to win our audience first.

It was a fantastic success. I was the prompter, and several times I saw an actor standing there helplessly, looking at me with clenched fists. Then I swiftly gave him a prompt. Once, the lover turned toward my prompter's box in the very middle of making his declaration of love and shouted out, "Wake up! Come on! Give it to me!" The audience exploded in gales of laughter because they thought that at long last the tongue of the stammering lover had been loosened and he was able to express himself clearly to Marishka!

I didn't remain in my prompter role for very long. I became fed up with standing in the prompter's box, looking through the little round window at the actors playing their roles. Immediately after the "tragedy" the group began rehearsing Andreyev's *The Seven Who Were Hanged*. After this production, the plan was to put on a Yiddish play. I learned all this from my barber, the small, agile Arontshik, after I stopped going to the widow's cellar.

Arontshik had also stopped performing in the theater. From day to day he became more unhappy and withdrawn. He stopped singing numbers from the Yiddish theater repertoire as he shaved my head. This was because he was in love with one of the fruit seller's daughters, a redhead with fiery cheeks. It was apparently a doomed love, for when she walked past the barber's she didn't even stop. She was in love with the porter's son, Artsho, who had played the role of the new lover in the tragedy.

It happened on a Sunday afternoon. The barber's shop was closed. The red-haired girl who had spurned the love of Arontshik was walking along the street. He stopped her, and both of them looked at each other without speaking. I was standing nearby, at the gate of my house, holding my breath as I watched what was happening.

Now Arontshik began, not speaking but screaming: "You have trampled on my heart! You have robbed me of sleep! My life no longer has meaning, for you are in love with another. We both must leave this world—now, this very moment!"

As soon as he had said these words, three shots rang out and a coil of smoke hung in the air between Arontshik and the girl. She fell on the cobblestones without making a sound.

Arontshik was taken to prison. There was a big funeral. I heard the girl's father say kaddish and the mother weep, and my heart ached, not so much from grief as from a feeling of personal guilt. When I encountered the director Fishl on the street the next day, he said to me: "It's really true, life is theater, and theater is, in fact, life . . ."

Getzl Okhlap

The front door of Reb Henekh Eyglitz's house was wide open, and harsh voices could be heard inside. Little groups of people gathered in the marketplace. The droshky drivers shook oats into the nosebags hanging from their horses' muzzles. The porters rubbed their hands and slapped each other on the back in a friendly fashion.

Getzl Okhlap's three sons were standing there shouting inside Reb Henekh's house:

"You lot have got us by the throats!"

"You want to bleed us dry!"

"You're going to make beggars of us . . . wandering peddlers!"

"We're being robbed in broad daylight!"

"We don't live in the jungle . . . we'll go to the *captain* . . ."

Reb Henekh, who was the head of the Burial Society, sprang up: "Whaaaat? You're threatening to inform on us? Get out of here, you young scoundrels! Get out!"

The three brothers backed away. They were short, red-faced, curly haired, bearded young men wearing unbuttoned short jackets and boots caked with mud, as if they had just come from the cattle shed. They remained on the steps with clenched fists, not knowing what to do.

"Get out!" screamed Reb Henekh. "Get out!"

The eldest of the three pushed both his brothers aside and took a few hasty steps back to the table where Reb Henekh was sitting.

"Please at least explain why these men are demanding such a fortune from us."

The head of the Burial Society twisted his pointed brown beard in his right hand.

"Why? Do you not know? Really? You poor, simple creatures . . ."

He started pacing with quick steps from one end of the room to the other, and each time he passed them he peered into the eyes of the three Okhlap brothers.

What was he to say to them?

Who didn't know of Getzl Okhlap's way of life? The whole community had been waiting for this moment for many years, and now the day of his earthly judgment had come. The town, after all, was not a lawless free-for-all, and his fate could serve as a lesson for others. He had never given any charity—neither money for the prayer house nor alms for the poor. During his lifetime the former stable lad had cut himself off from the Jewish religion and community, not through conversion but simply by avoiding Jews. Wherever there was a bar where goyim were boozing, that was where Getzl Okhlap was to be found. Even his clothes weren't Jewish; he wore a cap with a leather visor pulled down to his eyes and a short brown jacket with an aristocratic-looking braid, and he always carried a whip, even on the Sabbath. He gambled on Sundays in gentile bars and fathered illegitimate children in the surrounding villages, whom young peasant women, their mothers, would sometimes bring to his house. "Getzl, either take back this bastard you've given me or give me money," they clamored. He never gave them any money, for he wouldn't have had enough to pay them all, but he would let them have a horse from his stable, or a cow, or sometimes a calf. That was how he paid them off.

Now Getzl is lying on the floor of his house and his old buddies are going in and out, renewing the candles in the candlesticks.

People in the market are gossiping:

"How dreadful . . . there wasn't even a prayer shawl in the house."

"Even the candlesticks had to be borrowed from a neighbor . . ."

"Was he really a Jew? Worse than a Turk!"

"They say that Mosharn Golembiazh wants to take revenge on the Okhlaps. He can't forget his fight with the three sons . . ."

The oldest of Getzl's sons threw off his jacket and drew up a stool to Reb Henekh's table.

"Let's discuss this amicably. . . . It's been three days, and it's the summer. How long can a corpse lie in a house? Reb Henekh, don't listen to my brothers' angry words—they're upset. Our father is being shamed."

The head of the Burial Society burst out laughing: "Did your father ever feel any shame? You're just talking nonsense."

"Well, then why did you charge the richest man in the town, Kossman the miller, just one thousand zlotys? Eh? Where's the justice in that?"

"Why are you pleading with him?" exclaimed the youngest brother. "They just want to ruin us! Come on, we'll harness the horse and drive out of the town with our father. We'll find somewhere to bury him—trust us. Does it matter where a person ends up?"

"Get out, you heathen!"

The oldest sprang up, grabbed his youngest brother by the shoulders, and pushed him against the wall. "Shut up, Wojtek, or I'll kill you!"

There was a sudden silence, and the three brothers bent their heads. In the doorway stood some other members of the Burial Society.

Reb Henekh spoke: "Let me tell you why the community wants ten thousand zlotys from you. You see, the wealthy Kossman was a generous man during his life. He donated money to the Talmud-Torah and helped the poor. His burial plot actually cost one thousand zlotys, and all the plots around his have already been reserved—they were sold for a lot of money. Their price rose because it is an honor to lie near the grave of Kossman the miller. But now, you see, we have to ask ten times as much for your father's burial plot because the plots around his will be worth nothing. They'll fall into disuse because no one will want to lie beside Getzl Okhlap. So the Burial Society will be hit heavily. Therefore, we have to cover that loss now. . . . It works out to ten thousand zlotys; that's what we've calculated. Anyway, don't worry, you're not going to be ruined . . . you're not exactly poor men . . ."

They haggled until it was time for the afternoon prayer. The two younger brothers exited, the eldest remaining, and he eventually managed to make a deal.

"How much?" they asked in the marketplace.

"Eight—not a groschen less . . ."

The funeral took place in haste. At the sides of the road there were peasant women in black. Some of the innkeepers from the non-Jewish quarters came, as well as the Sunday card players. There were also coachmen and droshky drivers, as well as members of the Burial Society. The latter had organized a banquet for after the evening prayers—there would be something to drink.

Suddenly the church bell started to peal. At that time? What on earth? Some young lads prodded each other with their elbows and stifled their laughter. They knew that this was Mosharn's work. He had gotten the bell ringer of the church near the market drunk and told him that as soon as the body of Getzl Okhlap passed he was to ring the bell as loudly as he possibly could. Mosharn would give him a signal—he would let free three ravens that he had caught several days ago. When the ravens flew up, cawing for all they were worth, Janek the Crucifix started pulling on the bell rope.

The three Okhlap sons clenched their fists as they walked behind the coffin. They looked up and saw the ravens tied down by the tail and heard the peal of the church bell. They knew it was Mosharn's work, and they would get even after the required seven days of mourning were over. *But perhaps Reb Henekh had been right after all,* thought the eldest son as the pealing stopped.

They recited the kaddish, which Reb Henekh whispered in their ears word for word. The words, which were strange to them, came out haltingly from their mouths. They looked at the short trampled grass of the cemetery mound on which they were standing—a bare mound of yellowish, clayey earth. A feeling of shame and humiliation suddenly enveloped them, as a fire sweeps through a haystack. And when they heard the gravedigger begging the dead man's pardon, a searing grief pierced them.

The eldest son suddenly cried out: "Don't worry, Father . . . in a year's time we'll put up a headstone for you—it'll be really beautiful."

He started to weep, and as if on command, so did the other two brothers. They wept for their father's death because he had been more to them than a father—he had been their confidant: he had taught them to fight and to drink liquor straight, and he'd shown them all the tricks of horse trading. They wept from humiliation, and rage, that the community had extorted so much money from them and that their enemy Mosharn had played such a horrible trick on them with the ravens and the church bell.

The three brothers went home from the cemetery with heavy steps. Sparks flew from their hobnailed boots. Night came, with the prospect of a storm.

The Fallen Angel

In the little fruit-storage barn belonging to Marem the orchard keeper, the servant maid Feygl the orphan was in her third day of labor. The midwife had come and gone several times already, annoyed that the girl just lay there so quietly, without a single moan. "And she couldn't even find a more suitable place to give birth than that lowly barn, so dark that you have to use a kerosene lamp, even in the middle of the day." Silently, the women assisting at the birth fussed around like hens. They had brought some linen and basins of water, and they draped the corner where the servant girl lay with a sheet.

In the little marketplace some women sat on the steps till late in the night, calculating on their fingers the weeks and months that Feygl the orphan had still been working, trying to figure out the identity of her child's father.

Every few minutes another woman ran, her apron fluttering in the breeze, to Marem the orchard keeper's little barn. "Has it happened yet?" they asked each other in a whisper. "Can we congratulate ourselves yet?" And the women gave each other knowing smiles and looked at their husbands suspiciously.

However much they calculated and pondered, they came to no conclusion; Feygl was a quiet, shy girl whom no one had ever seen running around with boys. She had worked for several years in the service of the old rabbi, and when he died she stayed with his widow and worked for her, just for her modest subsistence. Every Friday morning she washed the floor of the prayer house and did not take any money for it.

"Perhaps it's the red-haired yeshiva boy from Łomża?"

"Or maybe Rokhem-Moyshe the water carrier?"

"Don't talk nonsense! It must be Yontl the dairyman!"

After midnight some of the bolder women went back to the little barn, carrying lanterns so that a bit of the street was illuminated as if it were broad daylight.

"Silly girl, there's nothing to be ashamed of. It's out in the open now anyway. Tell us who the father is. It will be better for the child and for you. After all, we live in a civilized society, and the man won't be able to wriggle his way out of it just like that. He has seduced you, poor thing, with fine words, promising you the moon . . ."

This was said by a woman with a broad, mannish face, who clenched her fists. The light of the lanterns illuminated the face of the girl in labor.

"She's really still just a child herself. Look how luminous she is. Like the saints in their pictures—like the Virgin Mary! Oh, it's terrible! Why don't you say anything, Feygl? You're burning with fever—look how she stretches out her hands. Someone run for the midwife!" But before the midwife arrived, the thin cry of a newborn baby was heard. It was a boy.

The women still pressed her for an answer to their question: "Tell us who the father is. Who is it? Is it the red-haired yeshiva boy? Rokhem-Moyshe? Yontl? Who is it?"

Feygl the orphan tried in vain to sit up. In the light of the kerosene lamp the women's hands stretched out to her, and the whispering that was coming from the courtyard gave her no peace. She longed to escape, to turn her face away from the firelight, to block her ears against the sharp words and snuggle her baby to her breast. And as the women moved ever closer to her with their hot bodies and burning breath, she jumped up from her bed of straw and began to scream: "You want to know who is the father of my child?"

The women were horrified by Feygl's burning eyes. "Oh, my God, how she has changed. This isn't the quiet little servant girl any more! She's more like someone from another world! A saint from another religion! Who is Feygl really?" And only now did the women remember that someone brought Feygl from somewhere abroad when she was just a baby and gave her to the old sock maker to bring up.

"You should know that the father of my child was an angel! A real angel from heaven!"

She died that same night, silently, like a lonely bird.

Feygl the orphan's son grew up among the market women. A pale little boy with fair, curly hair and a long face, he suddenly shot up and became very tall, like a plant that grows out of the darkness toward the brightness of the sky. He was different from everyone else. His voice was melodious, and it had a resonance like vibrating harp strings. He would fold his hands over his slender boy's chest, and he walked with a light, swaying gait.

One day one of the boys in the *kheyder* noticed that Feygl the orphan's son left no traces in the sand when he walked over it. This was told to the melamed, Reb Nosn. The boys were just learning their *khumesh*; they were studying the Book of Genesis and had just reached the chapter that tells the story of the fallen angels who descended from heaven to earth. The melamed translated from the Hebrew with a nigun: "And when the angels had come down from heaven onto the earth, they did see beautiful females, that is to say, women; therefore the angels of heaven knew them, and they had children."

As soon as the melamed had finished speaking, Henekh sprang out of his seat. He was the boy who had sworn that Feygl the orphan's son did not walk on the earth but hovered over it; the proof was that he left no traces of his footsteps. Henekh shouted at the top of his voice: "Rebbe, he is the child of a fallen angel! I swear it by the fringes of my prayer shawl! Rebbe, Feygl's son is a fallen angel!"

From that day on it began to be rumored in the town that the child of a fallen angel was living in their community. They again tried to find out who his father was, without success. Nor could they discover who Feygl the orphan really was. The women who had prepared her body for burial related that she had been as light as a feather, and while the earth was being scattered over her two wings had risen up and fluttered around her grave. Only now did they realize this was the angel who had slept with her . . .

By the age of eighteen, Henekh, the *kheyder* boy who was the first to notice the characteristics of an angel in Feygl's son, had become a great scholar. He studied together with several other yeshiva boys, and it was expected that he would become the rabbi of Przyborowice. Rich grain merchants were keen to have him as a son-in-law, and Yosefe the mikveh attendant did everything in her power to further these overtures, for Henekh was her longed-for only son.

One hot day in the summer month of Tammuz, Henekh closed the Book of Ezra and said to the other yeshiva students that he felt within himself a great vocation.

"I have heard a voice commanding me to search for one of the fallen angels and decree to him that he should spread his wings, which no mortal can see, and rise up above our earth. At that moment the Lord, blessed be He, will redeem us. And thus He did speak to me: 'It was not by chance that you were given the name *Henekh*. Once already I sent my minister, Henekh,[1] down to the fallen angels to persuade them to repent and to bring them back to heaven. You are a reincarnation of Henekh. Go and seek out Feygl the orphan's son and carry out this mission, Henekh.'"

Henekh wandered about the little streets where the artisans, the porters, and the fruit sellers lived. He went to Marem the orchard keeper and found her door padlocked. He was told that the fallen angel was a guardian in the orchards somewhere near the village of Glinojeck or perhaps Przyborowice.

In the prayer house, the market traders and sellers of farm produce said that Henekh wandered the roads with bare feet and tattered clothing, and that no matter how hard one tried to speak to him, he did not reply. He refused to get into a cart and be taken back to the prayer house. He lived on bread and water. This created turmoil in the shtetl, and people went out to search for the wandering Henekh.

---

[1] I.e., Enoch. Henekh is the Yiddish form of the name "Enoch."

The yeshiva students recounted Henekh's declaration word for word to the old rabbi. For three days the rabbi read through the books of Enoch and Baruch, as well as the fourth book of Ezra; then on the third day he called Henekh's mother to him and said to her: "It is the will of God. Do not be sad. Pray to God, and your child will return."

The meeting between Henekh and the fallen angel took place in a distant village between Wyszogród and Płock, in an old orchard. In the mountains, by the river Vistula, a relative of Marem's had an apple orchard. And because that year the harvest had been very meager, due to a violent wind from the mountains that had blown the fruit off before it was ripe, the fallen angel had been alone for the whole summer in this desolate place. The orchard keeper had not even thought of providing food for the guardian, but a peasant woman had brought him a bottle of milk and a few potatoes every day. Each time she caught sight of the young Jew, she crossed herself. He was as tall and straight as a young poplar, and he would stand for hours among the old trees, staring at the mountains. "You are tall enough to reach to heaven. You can stop the movement of the clouds with your hands," the pious Christian woman used to say to him.

Henekh fell down three times with his face on the grass in front of the angel. They purified their hands by washing them in the Vistula, and then they ate simple black bread, dipped in salt. When it began to get dark, both of them were deep in their prayers. The wind whistled wildly among the dry branches, tearing the spiders' webs tangled in the bushes. A flock of crows flew low and began to descend on the branches of the apple trees.

"Drive them away! They are evil spirits! Demons! They persuaded the angels to sin . . ."

The tall young man stood up and waved his hands, and the crows flew away in panic.

Deep into the night Henekh retold in detail the story of the four hundred angels who had rebelled in heaven against the Almighty and thereafter descended onto a mountain. This mountain was peopled with one of the most handsome human tribes that has ever existed on our earth. The women were wonderfully beautiful, well-formed, and charming. Therefore the angels could not withstand the temptation; they lived with the women, and children were born who were taller than all other human children. Their heads reached to the first heaven, and they could stop the movement of the clouds with their hands.

Feygl the orphan's son began to believe that Henekh's words were true.

The yeshiva student then revealed to him the secret that he, Henekh, was a reincarnation of the Henekh whom God Himself had sent to the fallen angels. That was why he, Henekh, had wandered barefoot, hungry, and thirsty around all the lonely roads of Mazovia in order to find the fallen angel and help him to recover his wings.

"You can get them back and fly up into heaven, and then we will all be redeemed. God will not be angry anymore, and days of blessedness will come for all of our people. I will be able to return in peace to the prayer house and become the rabbi of Przyborowice. If you hesitate, however—in other words, if you are unwilling to obey the command of Henekh who has come with this mission—I will roam the earth homeless, fasting or eating only crumbs of bread, and I will die. You see how demons plague me, how they lay stones in my path and expose me to temptation? Only your outstretched hand was able to drive away the black crows, because your strength is mighty, though you yourself are unaware of it."

Henekh's words in the middle of the night fell on the young man like dew. It was the first time anyone had ever spoken to him like a human being. He knew the words were true, because Henekh had been the one who, even as a young boy in the *kheyder*, had called out that he was a fallen angel.

Henekh spent three days and three nights in the old apple orchard with the fallen angel. What they talked about will remain an eternal secret because nothing could be gotten out of Henekh. The only thing that is known is that on the third night, when the clouds descended low over the mountains and drowned in the water of the Vistula, they both left the orchard and went to the high riverbank. From there they climbed onto a cliff. As Henekh prayed in a low voice he suddenly jumped up, crying out: "Now the moment has come for you to return to heaven. I see the signs! Wings are descending toward us—they are yours! Hurry and strip yourself naked! Generations are waiting for this wonderful moment. I, Henekh, call to You, the one and only God. Hear my call. I am obeying Your summons and fulfilling Your mission. Here I stand with the angel on the same mountain of sin! Help him to fly! Give him back his wings, for they belong to him."

The fallen angel hastily threw off his clothes and stood there naked.

"I see a light! The wings are fluttering above you! Do you see them?"

"Yes, I see them," said Feygl the orphan's son.

"Do you feel them on your body?"

"Yes, I feel them ... they have already attached themselves to me ..."

"Fly! I command you, I, Henekh, the one sent by God! Fly! Fly!" The angel jumped and disappeared in the mist.

The funeral of the fallen angel was sparsely attended because it was the high summer, the month of Tammuz, and the people were all busy in the orchards and in their villages. Henekh never came back again. He roams, homeless, around the melancholy roads of Poland.

The Last Scribe

It was an old prayer book wrapped in a prayer shawl, which lay in the cupboard beside the Sabbath candlesticks—a prayer book for the New Year, with a faded leather cover and yellowed pages. Three times in my life I have had the honor of holding and admiring it. Before describing those three instances, which are engraved on my memory, I should give further details about this remarkable volume, which we called the "genealogical prayer book." It was printed in Amsterdam about four hundred years ago. When open, it took up half the surface of the table. On one cover there was part of a silver clasp, but the other half was missing.

Its importance lay in the folded sheet of matte, silver-gray, light-grained parchment stitched to the inside of the front cover, which was only revealed when the book was opened. Drawn on it was a sturdy tree with dozens of subdivided branches and roots. On closer inspection, one could see that words had been delicately inscribed on the branches in all sorts of different inks.

My father, as the eldest son, had inherited this genealogical prayer book from his grandfather. My uncles were quite happy with this, although they were perplexed about one thing: Why was there such a rush? One might have expected this family heirloom to be passed on when my grandfather reached the proverbial age of one hundred and twenty! But at this point he still appeared, thank God, to be fit and well. So they saw his action as a sign that my grandfather was expecting something. And what this "something" was they all knew in their hearts but didn't want to say: they feared that their father's handing over of the book meant that his light was beginning to fade.

But let us return to the beginning; I would like to describe the three occasions on which I saw the New Year prayer book and even held it in my hands.

The first time I saw the book with the parchment sheet was at the time of my bar mitzvah, a year after my father had brought it home and laid it in the cupboard. Grandfather had come to Warsaw. From my little room I heard my mother saying quietly to my father, "Oh, dear! Father-in-law has really changed. I realize now that your brothers were right. He's aged, and his face is full of sadness. Old age has come upon him all at once."

I could say the week's Torah portion correctly, word for word. On the day of the bar mitzvah itself, when I was called up to read, every-thing went well enough—I received neither extravagant praise nor, thank goodness, severe criticism. My grandfather, however, shook his head sadly and said, "Hmph!" I didn't know what this "hmph" meant, but one of my uncles smiled good-naturedly and said to me: "Well, dear Mendele, you'll not end up as a cantor . . . nor as a preacher . . . and *certainly* not as a rabbi."

At this, Grandfather raised his head, and I was aware of his bushy gray eyebrows that met in the middle and his graying red beard, di-sheveled and stiff as parchment.

He spoke in a soft, hoarse voice: "You will be a scribe, Grand-son, a *sofer* ST'aM, as I and my grandfather and my grandfather's grandfather were. You will write with a goose quill pen. I shall teach you how to fashion it. Do you know what *ST'aM* means, my child? It means *sforim, tefillin, mezuzahs.* Repeat that after me, word for word . . ."

I repeated my grandfather's words quietly and saw his eyes fill-ing with tears.

That evening, after the close of the Sabbath, when Mother had wiped the misted windowpanes and said the prayer "God of Abraham, Isaac, and Jacob and of all our holy ancestors . . ." and the lamp had been lit, my father took a bunch of tiny keys out of his waistcoat pocket and opened the cupboard. Mother wiped the big table clean and covered it with a cloth. Father placed his folded prayer shawl on the table, and I noticed how his hands trembled as he opened the prayer book. It was then that I saw for the first time the big tree with the hundreds of names written on its branches.

Grandfather took a little case out of his waistcoat pocket. I thought it contained his spectacles, but how astonished I was when I saw goose quills and a little slim bottle of special ink. He and my father bent over the unfolded parchment, which consisted of several strips sewn together. Their lips quickly whispered the names inscribed there, their fingers moving from thick branches to thinner ones, and then to a little twig—until finally their fingers ceased moving. "There!" Grandfather said, dipping his goose quill pen into the little bottle. I heard the scratching of the pen on the parchment. My mother stood silently the whole time, and when Grandfather wiped his pen and placed it back in its little case, she came over to me quickly and kissed me.

"My child, may you have the honor of inscribing the names of your children and children's children here."

That evening I learned that in our family a boy's name was only inscribed on the family tree after his bar mitzvah, and his wife's name was added when he married. Because my grandfather sensed that his days were numbered and that he would soon be parting from all of us, he had made the long journey from Warsaw in order to inscribe, for the very last time, the name of a grandson who had become bar mitzvah.

I don't know whether my grandfather, may he rest in peace, had expressly asked my father to leave the two of us alone together or whether my father just left the room of his own accord. I only remember that he suddenly disappeared, and that my mother put two glasses of tea on the table, closed the door, and told everyone to be quiet. I saw her closing the shutters from outside, and I was overcome by the silence mingled with a secret feeling of awe. I was frightened of my grandfather and drawn to him at the same time.

"I want to talk to you. You are now an adult. Here is a tree spread out in front of you. Do you see its branches?"

"Yes, I see them."

"Let us start with the roots of the tree. One always starts from below, not from above. Remember that. A house—with the foundations. A tree—with the roots."

"I will remember it."

"Do you see the two forks of the root? The name *Menachem* is inscribed there. Now have a look at the name I have just written above, on the right-hand side."

I looked and saw the inscription "Menachem ben Zvi-Peysakh."

"Do you see how the names repeat themselves? From your slender branch another little branch will sprout, and you will inscribe new names there with your own hand. Amen, may it be so."

Grandfather took a sip of tea and continued: "One branch comes from Amsterdam. A great-great-grandfather received the call to be a scribe in Poznan and settled there. His children became scribes too and went to Lithuania, to the shtetl Radashkovichy, and another went to Węgrów, near Warsaw. The other branch also originates in those places. A great-grandfather on your mother's side was called to the Duchy of Mazovia, when Płock was the capital, in order to build windmills. He had learned the skill in Holland. And so one branch becomes interwoven with another. The family is scattered, and I am the last scribe. Take the goose quill pen, look at it. Go on, try now to write something!"

I tried, I wrote, and my grandfather was overjoyed. "Do you promise me that you will become a scribe?"

"I promise."

Grandfather stood up. He flung open the door and called for more tea, as we had let it get cold. For the three days of my grandfather's visit he taught me to make goose quill pens. I used up all the feathers of our dusters and ran around to the various aunts to get new ones. On the third day my grandfather left, and three months later the news came that he had died.

By the second time I opened the old prayer book, I had already become a scribe. Not the kind of scribe that my grandfather had wished me to be—the heir of a whole generation of scribes who had written Torah scrolls in their pure and careful handwriting, experiencing the word of God in every letter they inscribed. No, I became a scribe of the everyday words of ordinary people. In my early years as a writer I wanted to record the story of the many-branched tree in simple Yiddish words. I wanted to depict all the roots and branches and describe everything I had heard on that Sabbath night. So then I opened the book for the second time, looked at the silvery-gray parchment, wrote down names and dates, and wrapped the book up again in the old prayer shawl.

It was a turbulent time, just before the war, and I was drawn to the world of ordinary Jews, which was as agitated as a beehive scattered by a savage wind.

The third time I held the prayer book in my hands was when Nazi armies were marching through the devastated city of Warsaw. The night before I fled, I opened the sheet of parchment for the last time and contemplated the many-branched family tree. The last name written there was my own.

Yesterday is destroyed like a burned forest. I walk through it alone. In my memory the tree in the old prayer book lives on.

Glossary

Abu Kabir: a former Palestinian village near Tel Aviv that was depopulated and mostly destroyed during the war of 1948.

Adar: the twelfth month of the Jewish calendar, falling during the period February–March.

Adar Sheni: literally "Second Adar." The month of Adar occurs in February–March. In some years, a second month of Adar, consisting of 29 days, is added after Adar I, so that seasonal festivals stay aligned with the solar year (the Jewish year being based on the lunar cycle, i.e., shorter).

Amkho?: Hebrew. Literally "Your nation?" The phrase was used as a secret way of finding out if someone was Jewish, especially during and immediately after the Holocaust.

Apollonia: an ancient city and fortress situated on the coast near Herzliya. Built by the Canaanites, it was originally called Arsuf and was renamed Apollonia during the Hellenistic period.

arbe-kanfes: Hebrew. Literally "four corners." The ritual undershirt with tassels at the four corners worn by observant Jews. Also known as *tales kotn* in Yiddish or *tallit katan* in Hebrew.

Ashkelon: city on the coast, 36 miles south of Tel Aviv. There are ruins of ancient cities and Byzantine and Crusader churches at Ashkelon.

asking the dead man's pardon: an old Ashkenazic custom. When the burial is over, the gravedigger asks the dead person to forgive them if they have not carried out some aspect of the burial rites properly—the washing of the corpse, the carrying of the bier, the laying of the corpse in the earth, and the ritual of the funeral service—thus inadvertently dishonoring the dead person.

Bandera and Bulba: Stepan Bandera (1909–1959) and Taras Dmytrovych Borovets (1908–1981) were Ukrainian nationalist leaders. The latter was nicknamed Taras Bulba after the eponymous novel by Nikolai Gogol. In fact, Bulba-Borovets was criticized by Bandera for refusing to participate in the massacre of Poles in Volhynia in 1943.

Banderovtsy: Russian term for the Ukrainian nationalists who were followers of Stepan Bandera.

cholent: a slow-cooking stew that is prepared on Friday and eaten on Shabbat.

Dzika Street, Niska Street: streets in Warsaw.

goyim: Yiddish word for non-Jews, also used in English. Often pejorative.

goyish: adjective from *goy*.

Horyn River: in Volhynia, now northwestern Ukraine.

kaddish: a prayer that is central in the funeral service.

khamsin: a dusty, hot wind that blows from the Sahara between March and May.

kheyder: religious school for young children.

khumesh: the five Books of Moses, the Pentateuch.

kolkhoz: a collective farm in the Soviet Union.

krakowiak: a lively Polish dance from the Krakow region.

kurkar: a type of sandstone formed from fossilized sea sand dunes, forming deep ridges along the coast of Israel.

Liebknecht: Karl Liebknecht, born 1871, German socialist; together with Rosa Luxemburg he founded the Sparticist League and the Communist Party of Germany. Assassinated by Freikorps troops in 1919.

mame-loshn: Yiddish speakers often refer to the language as *mame-loshn,* literally "mother tongue."

Mazovia: the region of mid-northeastern Poland where Mendel Mann was born.

melamed: teacher in a *kheyder.*

minyan: a group of ten men, the minimum required to pray in a synagogue or prayer house. Also applied to the prayers themselves.

mikveh: ritual bath where religious Jewish women purify themselves every month.

Mikveh-Israel: the first agricultural college in Israel, established in 1870, southeast of Tel Aviv.

Mitzpe Ramon: a town in the Negev Desert in the south of Israel.

muzhik: a Russian peasant.

Nabateans: an ancient trading people with a highly developed culture who inhabited lands in the Middle East. Their existence in the desert was facilitated through a series of underground bottle-necked cisterns for rainwater. Their most famous architectural achievement is the city of Petra in modern Jordan, but there are also impressive Nabatean archaeological sites in modern Israel.

Nablus: a city on the West Bank; the biblical city of Shechem. Between

1948 and 1967 it was under Jordanian administration.

nigun: A melody. Also the chant used when reciting Biblical texts.

NKVD: The People's Commissariat for Internal Affairs; a Soviet law enforcement agency closely associated with the Soviet secret police.

Our Lady of Częstochowa: also known as the Black Madonna of Częstochowa; a four-foot-high icon of the Madonna, reputed to date from the fourth century, in the Jasna Góra Monastery in Częstochowa.

panienka: diminutive form of *pani*, Polish for "lady" or "madam."

Pilsudski: Josef Pilsudski (1867–1935), Polish revolutionary and statesman, head of state of newly independent Poland between 1918 and 1922.

pood: an old Russian measure of weight, equivalent to approximately 16.38 kilograms. It was officially abolished in 1924 but remained in popular usage until the 1940s.

Prophets Street: a street in Jerusalem.

rebbe: Hasidic leader or teacher.

Serkele: a well-known Yiddish play by Shloyme Ettinger (1803–1856). It was not published until 1861 and became a success in the early Yiddish theater.

"The Seven Who Were Hanged": a short story by the Russian author Leonid Andreyev, published in 1908. It was made into a film in 1920.

sforim, tefillin, mezuzahs: a holy book such as the Torah or Talmud is known as a *seyfer* (pl. *sforim*); phylacteries (*tefillin*) are the little leather cases containing holy texts that are bound onto the forehead and forearm when praying; mezuzahs are the small cases containing holy texts that are fastened to the door lintel of Jewish homes. ST'aM is an acronym made up of the first letters of these three Hebrew words (the "a" is added in English to reflect the pronunciation).

shtetl: a small town with a large Jewish population.

Talmud-Torah: a school where children were given an elementary education in the Pentateuch, the Talmud, and the Hebrew language.

Tammuz: the fourth month of the Jewish calendar, falling during the period June–July.

Tin'geshi: village in Chuvashia.

treyf: Jewish term for nonkosher food.

verst: an old Russian measurement of distance, just over a kilometer.

wadi: a steep-sided watercourse that is only full after heavy rainfall.

Author and Translator

Mendel Mann (1916–1975) was born in Płońsk, Poland. When World War II broke out, Mann was forced to abandon his plan to study art in Warsaw and fled to the Chuvash Soviet Socialist Republic, where he worked as a teacher before enlisting in the Red Army. His *War Trilogy*, published between 1956 and 1960, evokes his wartime experiences. He returned to Poland after the war only to discover that his whole family had been killed. In 1946 he moved to Regensburg, Germany, with his wife and small son, where he edited a Yiddish daily newspaper. The family emigrated to Israel in 1948, and Mann became editorial secretary of Avrom Sutzkever's influential literary journal *Di goldene keyt* (*The Golden Chain*). Mann's final homeland was France: in 1961 he moved to Paris to work for the Yiddish newspaper *Undzer vort* (*Our Word*). His literary work flourished there and he returned to his first love, painting, producing watercolors of great delicacy. He died suddenly at age 59. His son Zvi still lives in Israel. Mendel Mann's poetry, novels, and short stories draw on his own turbulent life but also vividly reflect and contemplate the various troubled strands of Jewish life and fate in the twentieth century.

Heather Valencia was a lecturer in German language and literature at the University of Stirling, Scotland. She began studying Yiddish in the 1980s, wrote her doctoral thesis on the poetry of Avrom Sutzkever, has published widely on Sutzkever and other writers, and has translated a wealth of modern Yiddish literature. Her published translations include Shmuel Harendorf's play *The King of Lampedusa* (2003), stories by Lamed Shapiro in *The Cross and Other Stories* (2007), the novel *Diamonds* by Esther Kreitman (2010), and a bilingual edition of Sutzkever's poetry, *Still My Word Sings* (2018). She has taught at Yiddish summer programs and teaches a Yiddish class in Edinburgh.

Acknowledgments

I am very grateful to Zvi Mann, the son of Mendel Mann, for permitting me to publish these translations of his father's work and for his constant encouragement of the project. I am indebted to Veronica Esposito and Eitan Kensky, whose painstaking editing and many good suggestions have been invaluable to me in arriving at the final version of the translations. Not least, I should like to thank the Yiddish Book Center for its interest in publishing the book, and in particular the excellent work of Lisa Newman and Madeleine Cohen on the design and production of the volume. Any mistakes or shortcomings are entirely my responsibility.

Heather Valencia

About the Yiddish Book Center

The Yiddish Book Center is a nonprofit organization working to recover, celebrate, and regenerate Yiddish and modern Jewish literature and culture.

The million books recovered by the Yiddish Book Center represent Jews' first sustained literary and cultural encounter with the modern world. The books are a window on the past thousand years of Jewish history, a precursor to modern Jewish writing in English, Hebrew, and other languages, and a springboard for new creativity.

Since its founding in 1980, the Center has launched a wide range of bibliographic, educational, and cultural programs to share these treasures with the wider world.

The Yiddish Book Center's Translation Initiative

The tens of thousands of books published in Yiddish contain untold treasures of literature, scholarship, memoir, and other unique documents that tell a rich and complex story of Jewish life in the modern world. Making these works accessible to English readers has become one of the Center's highest priorities, which is why the Center launched a multipronged translation initiative:

- publishing ten critically acclaimed translations of Yiddish novels, memoirs, plays, and journalism through the New Yiddish Library series at Yale University Press
- establishing a Translation Fellowship Program for training and mentoring a new generation of Yiddish literary translators
- bringing newly translated works to publication in the Yiddish Book Center's *Pakn Treger* magazine and its annual digital translation issue
- posting new works in translation on yiddishbookcenter.org

Recently Published by Yiddish Book Center Translation Fellows and Translations Prize Winners

On the Landing: Stories by Yenta Mash, translated by Ellen Cassedy (Northern Illinois University Press/A Yiddish Book Center Translation, 2018)

Judgment, by David Bergelson, translated by Harriet Murav and Sasha Senderovich (Northwestern/A Yiddish Book Center Translation, 2017)

Pioneers: The First Breach, by S. Ansky, translated by Rose Waldman (Syracuse/A Yiddish Book Center Translation, 2017)

Vilna, My Vilna, by Abraham Karpinowitz, translated by Helen Mintz (Syracuse University Press, 2016)

Attractive Hebrews: The Lambert Yiddish Cylinders 1901–1905, translated by Henry Sapoznik (Archeophone Records, 2016)

Oedipus in Brooklyn and Other Stories, by Blume Lempel, translated by Ellen Cassedy and Yermiyahu Ahron Taub (Mandel Vilar Press, 2016)

Forthcoming

Hibru, by Joseph Opatoshu, translated by Shulamith Berger (Ben Yehuda Press)

Warsaw Stories, by Hersh Dovid Nomberg, translated by Daniel Kennedy (A Yiddish Book Center Translation)

Honey on the Page: An Annotated Anthology of Yiddish Children's Literature, translated by Miriam Udel (NYU Press)

The Rabbi's House, by Chaim Grade, translated by Rose Waldman (Knopf)